The Snow Maiden

Best Wishes!
Joe Rogers

The Snow Maiden

A Suspense Thriller

Joseph P. Rogers

iUniverse, Inc.
New York Lincoln Shanghai

The Snow Maiden

A Suspense Thriller

iUniverse books may be ordered through booksellers or by contacting:

iUniverse
2021 Pine Lake Road, Suite 100
Lincoln, NE 68512
www.iuniverse.com
1-800-Authors (1-800-288-4677)

ISBN: 978-0-595-44644-5 (pbk)
ISBN: 978-0-595-68882-1 (cloth)
ISBN: 978-0-595-88968-6 (ebk)

Printed in the United States of America

"The winds of grace are always blowing, but it is you who must raise your sails."

—Rabindranath Tagore (1861–1941)

"Put out into the deep water and lower your nets for a catch."

—Luke 5:4

CHAPTER 1

Amidst the swirling snow and bustling crowd in the town square, a blonde young girl with a cherubic face pulled her wagon along as she moved forward with the determination of a treasure seeker who had just spotted a pearl of great price.

"Slow down, child!" her grandmother called to her, hurrying along the street as she attempted to keep pace with the girl.

"Yes, Gram." Chloe stopped long enough for her grandmother to catch up with her, then continued forward at a more moderate pace.

"Good girl." Few children would have obeyed so quickly, the grandmother reflected. I'm actually glad to see that she can walk so fast. Perhaps she is not as ill as the doctors think that she is. Dear God, let her live. I shouldn't outlive my granddaughter.

They stopped a few yards from the stage that was in front of St. Faustina Church.

It was almost sunset on New Year's Day as five young women competing for the title of Snow Maiden stood on the stage. They were the five finalists out of twenty contestants.

"Such beautiful young ladies. In about ten years or so, you'll be one of those contestants up on that stage."

Chloe knew that she would not, but she did not want to upset her grandmother, so she said nothing.

"Which contestant do you want to win?" her grandmother asked her in a conspiratorial whisper.

"That one!" Chloe replied without hesitation, pointing at a 22-year-old blonde named Sarah Hamilton.

"I can see why you want her to win," the grandmother said with a chuckle. "She looks like an older version of yourself."

"No, that's not why. I want her to win because she needs to win. And she will win because it is necessary."

"Are you having another of your visions, dear?"

"No, Gram. I sometimes just know things."

Her grandmother nodded. She had no doubt who was going to win the pageant.

However, none of the five nervous young women on the stage shared that certainty. While they awaited the judges' decision, they spoke quietly amongst themselves.

"I am freezing to death out here," Sarah said, hugging herself and bouncing up and down to try to generate some warmth. "What is taking the judges so long?"

Kara, a 22-year-old brunette, laughed. "Today isn't so cold. You've been away at college in California for four years. You have become used to that warm weather out there."

Sarah had been Kara's best friend since the two met during their freshman year in high school. They had both been cheerleaders and had both played on the tennis team.

However, they had ended up going to different colleges because Sarah wanted to attend a university in California that was not of interest to Kara. Kara wanted to major in communication disorders; Sarah's university did not offer that degree, so for their college studies, Sarah headed west while Kara headed east.

However, despite being on different coasts with a vast country between them, the two young women were able to maintain their friendship. They called or e-mailed each other almost every day. During Christmas and summer vacations, when they returned to visit their families, the two young women spent a lot of time together.

"I miss California and its nice warm weather. This is ridiculous."

"That's not a very good attitude for a Snow Maiden!" Tiffany said with a laugh.

"Well, this Snow Maiden is turning into ice," Sarah said.

"I think that you are saved," Holly said. "Here comes Mrs. Bentley with the decision."

Theodora Bentley had arisen from her chair at the judges' table and walked over to the nearby microphone at the podium.

She cleared her throat, then spoke to the crowd. "Ladies and gentlemen, I want to thank all of you for coming to our festival today. It has been a wonderful day. Our festival will conclude with the fireworks display that will begin in about a half-hour. As usual, St. Faustina parish has been our great host. I want to thank Father Kinsella and Father Dorsey for all their help."

The crowd applauded the two priests who stood on the steps of the church, which was directly behind the platform.

When the applause ended, Theodora continued, "As you can all see, we have five beautiful and talented finalists, so we had a difficult time reaching a decision. In truth, all of you are winners because the four runners-up will participate with the Snow Maiden at many events through the year." She ceremoniously raised an envelope, tore it open, and removed a slip of paper. "This year's Snow Maiden is Sarah Hamilton."

The crowd applauded as the four other contestants congratulated the winner.

"Thank you very much!" she said to the women as they hugged her. "I truly am surprised to win. For the last four years, I have only been back home here in this town during my vacations from school. I thought that would work against me."

"I've only been a part-time resident here the past couple of years myself," Tiffany said as she gave her a hug.

Theodora placed the silver tiara on Sarah's head. "We certainly have a beautiful Snow Maiden this year. I wish that I had naturally blonde hair like yours."

"Oh, I give my hair a bit of help to stay this blonde," Sarah admitted with a smile.

Theodora laughed. "Now don't any of you girls go running away. Chicago and Milwaukee and Madison television stations are sending reporters to do stories for their evening news. However, they have been delayed getting here by the heavy snow on the roads. They will be here before the fireworks display."

The five ladies agreed to wait for the television reporters; they all planned to stay to watch the fireworks display anyway.

The parents and a couple of friends of the newly-crowned Snow Maiden gathered around her and engaged in enthusiastic conversation for several minutes.

"I need to go inside somewhere and warm up so that I'm not an icicle when the television cameras get here," Sarah said, looking around for a sanctuary from the cold. "The church is open. I can get warm in there."

"Well, I'm glad that something can get you back into the church," her mother said with a long-suffering expression.

"Mother, let's not have that discussion again—especially not now."

"We'll meet you in the church in a few minutes," her father said. "That newspaper reporter who interviewed you and the other contestants this afternoon is waiting to interview us over by the pavilion. He wants the perspective of the proud parents."

"That's great. He has a good sense of humor. You'll enjoy talking to him."

"Let's hope that he writes a good story about you," her mother waved as they walked away.

CHAPTER 2

Sarah went up the front steps of the church, pulled open one of the heavy doors, and went into the vestibule where she had intended to wait. However, she was surprised to see that all of the lights were on in the church, and there were a few persons in the pews.

Curious she went through the doorway into the church, ignoring the holy water font at the entrance. She walked over to the side wall and began to admire the beautiful stained glass windows depicting the mysteries of the rosary. I think that this is the first time that I have looked at these closely, Sarah reflected as she gazed at a window showing a Nativity scene.

"Ah good, I wasn't sure whether anyone would come to confession this evening," Father Kinsella said as he walked up to her.

"What?" Her attention had been so focused on the windows that she had not seen the priest approaching her. "Oh, hello, Father." She tried to recall his name. "Confession?"

Sarah suddenly realized that she was standing directly next to one of the two confessionals in the church. She noticed that two crosses were illuminated outside the other confessional, indicating that both a priest and penitent were inside.

"I assumed that you are here for the sacrament of penance, but perhaps I am mistaken," Father Kinsella said, seeing her surprised reaction.

"To tell you the truth, I just came inside to get warm, but since I'm here anyway, let's go ahead with a confession."

"Very good."

He opened the wooden door, and they both went into the room. As he walked around to other side of a screen, Sarah glanced at the cushioned kneeler in front of the screen and then looked over at the second chair on his side of the screen.

Momentarily confused, she stood there motionless. "I haven't been to confession in many years, Father. Am I supposed to kneel there or sit in the chair?"

"Whichever way you are more comfortable will be fine. You have the option of face-to-face confession in the chair or receiving the sacrament anonymously by kneeling behind the screen."

"My anonymity is pretty much already blown, so I guess that I might as well just sit in the chair."

The priest chuckled. "Very true. And I would recommend not wearing the sparkling tiara if you want to remain anonymous."

Her hands went instantly to the tiara. "Oh my gosh, I forgot that I still had that thing on! I look like such a diva!" She removed the tiara and placed it in her lap as she sat down across from the priest.

"Okay, let's get started. God is glad that you are here."

What on earth am I doing here, Sarah suddenly wondered. I should just leave.

Noticing her hesitation, the priest continued, "You mentioned that it has been quite a while since your last confession. How long has it been?"

"I'm 22 years old. I was in the eighth grade when I made my last confession, so I guess it has been about nine years."

"All right. What sins did you commit during those nine years?"

"This is really weird. I don't feel like telling you." She glanced toward the door. "There are several persons seated in the church. Someone could overhear us."

"These confessionals are designed to muffle sound. As long as you keep your voice at a moderate level, no one outside can overhear. A couple of minutes ago you were only a short distance from the other confessional in which someone was speaking to Father Dorsey. I'm sure that you couldn't hear what they were saying."

"I didn't hear anything," Sarah admitted. "However, you can hear me. How do I know that you won't tell anyone?"

"It would be a mortal sin for me to repeat to anyone anything that I hear in confession. In addition, I would be excommunicated from the Catholic Church. Throughout all of history, there are very few instances of priests betraying the confidentiality of this sacrament."

"That sounds good, but I would bet that under enough pressure, you would reveal what someone told you."

Father Kinsella shook his head. "No, not even if the court ordered me to do so. I would go to prison for the rest of my life rather than reveal what someone told me."

"What if I told you that I plan to stab Father Dorsey to death after we finish speaking? What if I said that I'm going to walk into his confessional and plunge a knife into his heart?"

"I would physically attempt to protect Father from any attacker, but I would not tell Father about a threat someone made against him during confession. I would do my best to discourage the person from carrying out any violence."

"I am not easily dissuaded, Father," she said with a sly grin. "Once I make up my mind to do something, I'm almost unstoppable."

"I assume that we have been speaking theoretically, and that you don't plan to murder our pastor?"

Sarah laughed softly. "No, Father is in no danger from me. I don't even know the man. I have been to a few of his Masses over the past several years."

"Have you been practicing your faith in recent years?"

"Not really. In high school, I would only go to Mass when my parents made me. We used to fight about it all the time. Sometimes, just for the sake of keeping peace in the house, I would give in and go to church with them. Sometimes my parents got tired of nagging me and let me stay home. For the past four years, I have been going to college in California. I never once went to Mass there. When I came home for vacations, I would come to Mass here with my family. We were at Midnight Mass on Christmas Eve. We got there a half hour early in order to hear the choir sing carols before the Mass began. It was very nice."

"I love to hear our choir sing Christmas carols," Father agreed. "Well, let's get back to your confession. What were your sins over the last nine years?"

"You are just determined to hear about how naughty I have been, aren't you? Very well. I have been a bad, bad girl."

"Go ahead."

"I committed fornication many times with different men. I also stole money—a lot of money. If I have shocked you, Father, I can wait until you recover."

"You would be surprised by how little shocks me. As a priest, I hear every imaginable sin confessed. As it says in Ecclesiastes, 'There is nothing new under the sun.'"

"I guess not. However, I doubt that anyone in this small town stole money the way that I did. I would meet men in bars and then slip a drug into their drinks. As soon as I got them outside, my boyfriend and I would steal their wallets and leave them unconscious on the sidewalk. We'd use their credit cards as quickly as possible to buy expensive jewelry and electronics. And, of course, we would take all of their cash."

"Why did you do this?"

"I needed money. Living in California is very expensive. My parents paid most of my tuition and my room-and-board, but I needed a lot more money for nice clothes and for drinking and partying. My boyfriend and I liked to go to Las Vegas sometimes on the weekend. We would pull the same scam there. We would wander through casinos looking for some high rollers who were winning big money. Then I would flirt with them and get them to buy me a drink. While the guy was looking at me, my boyfriend would slip the pill into his drink. It worked like a charm."

"What drug did you and your boyfriend use on them?"

"GHB or roofies—They are considered 'date rape' drugs."

"I have heard that those drugs are very dangerous. Some women have gone into comas and died after being given those drugs."

"No one died, Father. At least I assume that no one did. After we left the men on the sidewalk, I never saw or heard about them again.

I'm sure that they were fine after they woke up. They just had a bit less money than before they went to sleep."

"If you know or can find out the identity of any of these men, you have an obligation to make restitution of any money that you stole from them."

"I only recall the first names of a few of the men. It would be impossible for me to find them again."

"I understand. Well, you can continue listing your sins."

"I'm sure that there's a lot more, but I'd have to think about it for a while, Father, and I really need to get going. I'm going to be on television later tonight. Everyone wants to see the sweet, innocent little Snow Maiden."

"Very well. Over the next few days I would encourage you to make an examination of conscience. It is especially important to try to recall all of your mortal sins. Then come to confession again to either me or to Father Dorsey. You receive grace every time that you receive the sacrament of penance."

"Yes, Father. I will try to do better." If I tell him what he wants to hear, I can get out of here faster.

"Do you recall how to say the 'Act of Contrition' prayer?"

"No, Father."

"You can say it along with me. "O my God, I am most heartily sorry for all my sins because I dread the loss of Heaven and the pains of Hell, but most of all because I have offended Thee, my God, who art all good and deserving of all my love. I firmly resolve, with the help of Thy grace, to sin no more and to avoid all occasion of sin."

The priest made the sign of the cross saying, "I absolve you of your sins in the name of the Father and of the Son and of the Holy Spirit. For your penance, try to begin saying some prayers on a regular basis and do some acts of kindness and charity for other persons."

When Father Kinsella stood up, Sarah did also. "Go in peace," he said. "Congratulations on being selected as the new Snow Maiden."

"Thank you, Father," she said, moving toward the door. "Have a good evening."

"Thanks, you too," he said.

Sarah walked out the door, across the church, and out into the vestibule. I guess that I didn't shock him as much as I thought I would, she reflected. He seemed to still like me even after hearing about those things that I did.

She went back out into the winter night. As Sarah descended the steps, she noticed a young man looking up at her. He was average looking and of about average height and weight. His brown hair was disheveled by the wind.

"Hi," he said warmly.

"Hi," she replied. "You look familiar, but I can't think of your name," she said.

"I'm Tom Angelique. I was two years ahead of you in high school. I used to see you in the hallways and around the campus sometimes."

"Oh, yes." Sarah looked at him intently, scanning her memory. "You acted in some of the plays."

"That's right." He looked pleased. "To tell you the truth, I'm surprised that you remember me."

She smiled. "I liked our high school plays. A couple of times I almost auditioned, but I was always so busy with cheerleading and some other activities that I never found the time."

"I wish that you had auditioned. Perhaps we could have co-starred together."

"Maybe that would have happened!" she said with a smile.

"Sarah, there you are!" Theodora Bentley called to her from the street. "I have been looking all over for you! Two of the television crews are here. I have rounded up the other girls, and we're waiting for you!"

"Coming, Mrs. Bentley. Tom, I have to go. It was great seeing you again."

"It was great seeing you, too. Congratulations on being the new Snow Maiden. I was rooting for you!"

"Thank you," she said, hurrying toward Theodora. "Bye!"

After finishing television interviews with news crews from Madison, Milwaukee, and Chicago, she stood on a hillside with her parents and watched the fireworks display with them. The crowd especially liked the grand finale, which included skyrockets fired low in the sky and in such rapid succession that everyone could feel the ground shake from the explosions.

"I'm meeting some friends to celebrate," she told her parents as they walked along with the departing crowd. She handed her tiara to her mother. "Will you take this home for me? Everyone will think that I'm an egomaniac if I keep wearing it around. I'll be home in a couple of hours."

"Don't stay out too late, dear," her worried mother said. "And make sure that no one drinks and drives."

"Yes, Mom. I'll see you both later." She rushed off.

She walked around the corner and approached a young man who was waiting for her beneath the canopy of a storefront.

"Hi dude."

"Hey, baby, well look at you—the little Snow Princess."

"Snow Maiden," she corrected him.

"Snow Whatever. If you are not a princess, nobody is."

"I guess that's a compliment, so thanks."

"I saw you come out of the church earlier this evening. Who was the gay guy who was talking to you on the steps?"

"What makes you think that he is gay?"

"He looked gay to me."

"Every guy that I talk to looks gay to you."

"Well, he looked especially gay."

"You are so ignorant."

"You didn't answer my question: who is he?"

"What do you care?"

"Just curious."

"He's just a guy that I went to high school with. He wanted to congratulate me."

"Isn't that sweet?" Wayne said mockingly.

"Actually, it is."

"I still think that he's gay."

"Has it occurred to you that if a man comes up to talk to me because he finds me attractive that he is probably not gay?"

"I don't know whether he's gay or not, but I'm sure that he is a loser."

"Do you losers have some way of recognizing each other?"

"Ow, baby. You are mean tonight. I thought that you would be in a good mood after winning your little crown."

"Talking to ignorant persons puts me in a bad mood."

"Is your gay, loser boyfriend also ignorant?"

"Just drop it. I barely know the guy. If he is a loser, he is a very wealthy loser. His family owns Angelique Plastiques, which is one of the largest companies in Wisconsin."

"Really? Very interesting."

"Why?"

"This guy might be a prime target for one of our scams. We could make a lot of money!"

"This is my hometown!" she declared angrily. "We are not scamming anyone here! We can do that in Los Angeles or Las Vegas, but not in my hometown!"

"All right! Calm down! And keep your voice down. There are still some people walking down this street." He hugged her. "I'm sorry, baby. Just forget it. Let's go have a drink. I found a good bar on the next block."

"I'm kind of tired. I'm just going to go home."

"I thought that we would go back to my motel room after we had a couple of drinks."

"No. Not tonight."

"Are you mad at me?"

"No. Everything's okay. It's just been a long, busy day. I'll meet you for lunch at noon tomorrow at the diner next door to that motel where you're staying."

"Okay, goodnight baby," he said and gave her a long kiss before they went their separate ways.

After watching the fireworks display, Chloe and her grandmother stopped by a few more carnival booths before they shut down. They won a few small prizes and purchased several other items.

"I think that is quite enough loot for one day, young lady."

"Yes, Gram."

They walked toward their car which was parked near the corner.

"I know that you are going to give most of it away to the other children at the hospital, but please keep at least one or two things for yourself."

The grandmother opened the trunk and placed the wagon and its contents inside.

"I will never understand how you knew which young woman would be the Snow Maiden."

"Sarah won because it was necessary for her to win in order for everything to work out right, the way that things are supposed to happen."

"You are truly an amazing child," the grandmother said.

CHAPTER 3

As Sarah had promised, the next day she walked into the diner almost exactly at noon. Wayne was already seated in a booth by the front window.

"Over here, baby" he waved to her.

"I wish that you would cut back on that 'baby' stuff. I do have a name, you know."

"Okay, okay, Sarah. How's it going today?"

"Pretty good. I have been getting a lot of congratulatory phone calls and e-mails."

"That's great. I have some good news myself. I found an apartment about two blocks from here. Staying in a motel was starting to get expensive, so I'm glad to get out of there."

"Is the apartment furnished?"

"Yeah. It's a nice place. The apartment complex has a workout room and an outdoor pool."

"That outdoor pool isn't going to do you much good at this time of year," she said with a grin.

"It's too bad that I can't just live at your house. Your bedroom would be big enough for both of us."

"Oh, yeah, that idea would go over well with my parents," she said sarcastically.

"I'm kind of insulted that you haven't even told your parents about us. They don't know that I'm in town."

"They don't even know that you exist."

"Thanks a lot. You sometimes make me feel like dirt."

"There isn't any point to telling them about you or having them meet you. They would despise you, and you would find them so religious and so prim-and-proper that you would make fun of them. I would get mad at you, and we would have a big fight. I can keep the peace by keeping you away from them."

"You might have a point there," he conceded.

They ate hamburgers, French fries, and shakes for lunch. After finishing their meals, she went back to the motel with him and then went over to see his new apartment.

When she returned to her house at about five o'clock that afternoon, she was greeted by the delicious smell of dinner cooking.

"Oh, that smells great!" she called to her mother. "What are we having for dinner?"

"I have a pot roast and potatoes cooking. It will be ready in about a half hour when your father gets home."

"Yum. Yum." Sarah sat down on the sofa in the living room.

Her mother came into the room. "You'll never guess who called while you were out," she said, smiling broadly.

"The President of the United States? The Queen of England?" Sarah joked.

"No, but he probably is wealthier than either of them. That adorable Thomas Angelique called you!"

Sarah's eyes widened with surprise. "I spoke with him briefly last night shortly before the fireworks display. I never expected him to call me, though."

"He is a wonderful actor and so cute! Last year he starred in a couple of community theater productions. I think that he will be a Broadway star someday."

"What did he want?"

"He didn't say, but I would assume that he wants to ask you out on a date."

"I barely know him."

"He is a very nice young man and comes from a prominent Catholic family. He'd be a wonderful catch."

"I don't know. He seems all right, but I'm not attracted to him." Sarah picked up a magazine from the coffee table and began casually paging through it.

"After you get to know a person better, you often develop some feelings of attraction for that person."

"Does he want me to call him back?"

"He said that he would call you again this evening."

"I'm planning to go out after dinner. I can't sit around all evening waiting for his phone call."

"Then call him back now or before you go out this evening. Sarah, if he asks you out, please accept the date. You aren't dating anyone else, and there is no reason for you to decline."

"I don't know."

"Give him a chance. It can't hurt anything."

"We'll see." She raised the magazine and pretended to be very interested in an article.

With a sigh, her mother returned to the kitchen.

After dinner, Sarah took her cell phone up to her bedroom and called the number that her mother had written on a slip of paper.

"Hello," a male voice answered.

"Hi, could I please speak to Tom?" she asked.

"This is Tom. Is this Sarah?"

"Yeah. Hey, what's up? My mom said that you called this afternoon."

"Yes. Well, how did your first day as Snow Maiden go?"

"It's kind of like a dream. I still can't believe that I won."

"Oh, you were definitely the right choice. I'll bet that the judges vote wasn't even close."

"Thanks."

"Sarah, the reason I called is that next Saturday evening the country club is having its annual Winter Ball. It's really a nice event. I'd like to invite you to go with me."

She hesitated for a moment, then said, "That sounds like fun, Tom. I'd love to go."

"Great. It will be an honor to have the Snow Maiden as my date. And I think that you will have a good time."

"I will look forward to it."

They spoke for a couple of more minutes before saying good-bye. Sarah went down to tell her parents the news that her mother had been eagerly awaiting.

Four days later Sarah was in O'Malley's Pub downtown. She was seated at the bar on a stool next to her boyfriend.

Wayne nudged her, gesturing with his head toward a middle-aged man in an expensive suit. Slouching in his chair at a table, the man was clearly intoxicated.

"That guy looks like he has money," he whispered to Sarah. "He would be an easy mark."

"No," she replied firmly.

"Come on," he cajoled her. "I know that this is your hometown, but let's just rob this one guy. I have a roofie in my pocket, but we might not even need to use it. He looks like he's going to pass out at any time. Just get friendly with him and offer him a ride home."

"No," she said a bit louder, getting annoyed.

"Listen, baby, we'll be doing a public service. We can keep a drunk driver off the roads; we might be saving some lives. Taking his money will just be our service fee."

"You are unbelievable. We can drive him home, but only on the condition that his wallet and its contents get home with him."

"Damn! Being back here in this town has made you into a prissy little angel!" he said without trying to whisper, causing the bartender to glance over at them.

"Hey, we noticed that man is in no condition to drive," Sarah said to the bartender. "Does he have a ride home?"

"He doesn't need one," the bartender said. "He walked over here. He lives in a condo just about a block away."

"Oh, that's good," Sarah said.

"We could walk him home and rob his condo after he passes out in bed," Wayne whispered to her.

Sarah placed several dollars on the bar. "Thank you. Goodnight," she said to the bartender and walked toward the front door.

"Baby," Wayne called to her, but she ignored him, went outside, and kept walking.

A few seconds later he came running up to her. "Where are you going, baby?"

"Home."

"Slow down. I'm sorry. I get the point. I won't try to get you to help me rob any of the good citizens of this town."

She looked sternly at him. "I don't want you to rob them either."

"Okay, I won't. Listen, why don't you and I drive to Chicago this weekend? We could have a great time there. There are some great restaurants and nightclubs. We could party all weekend and maybe make some money. At least I guess that it's okay with you if we pull our scam on a few people in Chicago."

"I can't go to Chicago this weekend. One of my duties as the Snow Maiden is to attend the Winter Ball at the country club. It's being held this Saturday evening."

"Damn! I was looking forward to going to Chicago. Can't you get out of going to this stupid event?"

"No, it's quite important."

"Just call them on Friday and say that you have the flu and will be too sick to go. One of those four other girls that you beat could take your place."

"This is my first official event as the Snow Maiden. It would look bad for me to miss the first event; the judges might think that they made the wrong choice."

"Aw, come on, who cares what they think?"

"I might be able to skip one or two events later this year, but not this first one. I'm not going to argue about this. Why don't you just go ahead and go to Chicago by yourself?"

"Aren't you worried that I will cheat on you there?"

"No, I doubt that any women there will be interested in you. I've heard that Chicago women have good taste in men. I wish that I did."

"Damn, you are cold! No wonder they made you the Ice Princess!"

"I am the Snow Maiden. This is probably the twentieth time that I have corrected you about my title. They should elect you the Idiot King."

"Go to Hell!" he exclaimed.

"When I'm with you, I am in Hell," she said, got in her car, slammed the door, and drove away.

Damn her, Wayne thought as he turned to walk back to the bar. I need one more drink before I head home, he reflected. As he was approaching the bar's entrance, the intoxicated man in the suit came staggering outside. This is too easy, Wayne thought with a sly grin.

"Let me help you out there, dude," he said as he steadied the man by holding his arm.

"What? Hey, thanks," the man said, surprised by the sudden appearance of this companion.

"No problem."

"I might have had one drink too many."

"Yeah, that's happened to me plenty of times."

They walked together for just over a block and went into the condominium building. As the man fumbled with the keys to the front door of his condo, Wayne reached out and took the keys from the man.

"Let me get that door for you," Wayne said and unlocked the door.

In spite of his inebriated condition, some sixth sense suddenly alerted the man to danger. "Hey, I'm fine now. Thanks for helping me out. I'll see you later."

"Okay, see you later, dude," he said and pretended that he was about to walk away so that the man wouldn't shout for help.

As he started to turn, Wayne sucker punched the man in the back of the head, grabbed the man by the shoulders, and shoved him into the condo. The man landed face down on the floor. Wayne stepped in after him and shut the front door.

The man was unconscious on the floor. He removed the man's wallet from his jacket pocket and examined its contents.

"Five hundred dollars. Jackpot." He looked down at the man. "What do you do for a living? Hmm, not very talkative, are you?"

He removed two credit cards from the wallet. None of its other contents looked useful, so he placed it back in the man's jacket pocket.

Going through the pockets in the man's pants, Wayne found some more cash.

"I'm glad that Sarah didn't come with me. I would have had to split this with her," he reflected to himself as he dragged the man into the bedroom.

Wayne roughly placed the man into the bed. When he wakes up in bed, he might not realize for a while that he has been robbed. That will give me more time to use his credit cards.

He made a quick search of the apartment and found some more cash, an expensive wristwatch, and a few other small items that he liked. Wayne opened some dresser drawers and looked beneath the clothing.

In one drawer, beneath a stack of shirts, he found an expensive Glock pistol. "This is my lucky night. I should buy some lottery tickets. In fact, I'll use his credit cards to buy them." He chuckled as he placed the gun into the pocket of his jacket.

Wayne was anxious to begin making purchases with the credit cards, so he did not want to linger in the apartment too long.

"Thanks, dude," he laughed at the unconscious man just before leaving the condo.

Chapter 4

That Saturday evening Tom Angelique picked up Sarah at her house and drove her to the country club.

"My mom is very impressed with your skills as an actor, Tom," she told him as they went past a golf course. "She has seen the plays that you did recently with the community theater group."

"Oh, thanks. I enjoy working with that theater group. This summer we are planning to have a Shakespeare Festival in Carondelet Park. If the festival goes well, we will make it an annual event."

"That should be great."

"Yeah. We have found the perfect place in the park to hold it. Near the art museum, the hillside forms kind of a natural amphitheatre where we can stage the plays. We are going to have a pre-show every evening starting at about six o'clock. It will run for about two hours until the play starts at 8:00 p.m."

"What is a pre-show?"

"There will be a bunch of different activities that persons who arrive early can watch. We're going to have a couple of professors or graduate students give lectures about Shakespeare. There will be strolling musicians, Renaissance dancers, and probably a magician strolling the grounds."

"Oh, I like magicians. Last year I saw a great magic show in Las Vegas. The magician was a woman, and she seemed to make doves appear out of thin air. I can't figure out where she had all those doves hidden."

"Those magicians are very clever. Last year I learned the hard way not to sit in the front row at a magic show. The magician brought me up onto the stage with him to help him with a trick. I examined several metal hoops to make sure they were solid. They looked solid to me, but he was able to make them pass through each other and link them all together."

"At least he didn't saw you in half," Sarah joked.

"Yes. Thank God for that!" Tom laughed.

He pulled the car into a parking space on the lot near the clubhouse. Sarah looked over at a man who was placing his golf clubs in the trunk of his car.

"Good grief! How could anyone play golf with several inches of snow on the ground?" she laughed.

"He was probably just using the indoor driving range. It's pretty cool. You are driving into a large net about ten yards in front of the tee, but there is a screen on which they project the images of a golf course. Based on how well you hit the ball, you see where it would land on the fairway or the green."

"It sounds like playing a video game."

"Yes, and it's a great way to improve your golf game, especially during the winter. The golf course simulator can let you play on several of the most famous courses like Pebble Beach and Augusta."

"I'm going to have to give that a try," Sarah said as they went into the clubhouse.

Three hours later, as Sarah came through the front door, her father was seated on the sofa in the living room watching television.

"Well, there she is—the belle of the ball." He turned down the volume on the television.

"Hi, Dad." She hung her coat in the hall closet.

"Did you have a nice time?"

"Yes. The country club was beautifully decorated. I have never before seen so many poinsettias. And everyone was so elegantly dressed."

"How was Tom?"

"Oh, he's very nice. He has a good sense of humor."

"Do I hear the distant chime of wedding bells?"

Sarah smiled. "No. I like him, but not romantically. I just want to be friends with him."

"When I was a single young man, I heard that line several times. It is not something that a man likes to hear from a beautiful young lady."

"Hey, you did all right for yourself." Sarah sat down on the sofa next to him, kicking off her high-heeled shoes. "Mom was quite a catch."

"Indeed she was. You might be surprised to hear that she was one of the women who told me that she just wanted to be friends."

"Really?"

"For several years, we were friends, and that was fine. I was very glad, though, when she eventually realized that I had some of the qualities that she wanted in a husband. Friendship is a great foundation on which to build a romance."

"Hmmm. Well, it worked out for you, but I'll have to think about that one." She stood up and walked toward the kitchen. "I'm going to get some milk and cookies. Do you want anything?"

"No, thanks."

"Has Mom already gone to bed?"

"Yes. She wanted to wait up for you, but she was feeling a bit too tired."

Sarah started to head into the kitchen, but then paused. "Why was she so tired?"

He hesitated for a moment, then said, "When you get to our age, you won't need to ask that question, young lady. Neither your mother nor I have the energy of someone your age. I'm going to be 60-years-old next month. I can't believe it!"

"I know that you are looking forward to retirement, Dad. Are you still planning on taking early retirement at 62?"

Again he paused before speaking. "Oh, I'm not sure what I'm going to do then. That is still quite a way in the future."

"There is something that you are not telling me, Dad."

"What makes you think that?"

"My sixth sense."

"Before you went to school in California, you only had five senses."

"They gave me an extra one out there. It was California's graduation present for me."

"I guess that explains it." He rolled his eyes.

"Come on. Let's hear it. What aren't you telling me?"

"You'd better fine tune that sixth sense of yours, young lady. There's nothing for you to worry about. I thought that you were going to get yourself some cookies and milk?"

"I'm not that easily distracted, Dad. Come on. Tell me what's up?"

He sighed. "Your mother would kill me. She wanted this to be a perfect, fantasy evening for you. Why don't we just wait and talk about this tomorrow?"

"Like I'm not going to worry now!" she declared. "Do you think that I could sleep without knowing what you are not telling me?"

"Okay, okay. You would be imagining that things are a lot worse than they actually are. I might as well just go ahead and tell you."

"Right."

"I hope that I won't be ruining your fantasy evening."

"There was nothing special about this evening. I just attended a fancy party. I have been to fancy parties in the past and will be going to other fancy parties in the future."

"I suppose so."

"Dad, you're procrastinating."

"Procrastinating. That's a good fancy word for you to use at your fancy parties."

"Dad! Tell me the news!"

"All right. Here's the story: two days ago I got laid off. The company didn't get the contract that they were expecting to get, so they had to lay off about thirty employees."

Sarah went over to the sofa, bent down, and hugged him. "I'm sorry, Dad."

"Thanks."

"You'll find another job soon."

"Hopefully, but at my age it might be tough. Now I won't receive any pension from the company when I turn 62. I have applied for unemployment compensation and will be getting that for a while."

"Yesterday and today you left the house and returned home at the same time that you always did when you were working. Where did you go all day?"

"Well, your mother and I didn't want you worrying. I just went over to the public library and read most of the day."

"Dad, you didn't need to do that! You and Mom treat me like such a baby!"

"It was no problem; I enjoyed spending some time in the library. I checked out a couple of good mystery novels. In addition, while I was walking around downtown, I noticed that a couple of the shops have "Help Wanted" signs in the windows. If I don't find a better-paying job in the next couple of months, I might just take one of those jobs."

"That would be an option to consider."

"Yes, but I'm sure that they don't pay much and probably don't offer any medical plan. Losing our family's medical coverage is probably the worst part about getting laid off at this time."

"Why is this time worse than any other time?'

He sighed again. "Your mother is going to kill me for telling you all of this tonight."

"Come on. Let's hear it."

"Your mother's cancer is no longer in remission. The doctor believes that her chances of survival are very good, but it is important that she continue to receive treatments—very expensive treatments. We have some savings, so we should be okay for a while.

However, we might eventually have to sell the house in order to pay for her healthcare."

Sarah was crestfallen. "Dad, you and Mom have lived in this house for almost 25 years. This is the only house in which I have ever lived. You don't want to sell it."

"Don't worry, Sarah. We might not need to sell. The hospital might succeed in knocking out the cancer before our savings run out. Or I might be able to find a job that will be good enough to keep paying for her treatments."

"I should be earning some money soon, Dad. I will try to help out."

"Everything will work out as it should, Sarah. Just say some prayers every day for your mother and for our family."

"I will." She stood up. "Now I'm going to get those cookies and milk. Are you sure that you don't want some?"

"Positive."

As she walked into the kitchen, an idea occurred to her, and she began to formulate a plan. Sarah realized how she could gain access to a lot of money in a short period of time. Neither of my parents would approve of this plan, she realized. In fact, they would be shocked. I cannot even hint to them what I am doing. My experience conning those men in California should be very helpful in implementing my plan.

Sarah sat down at the kitchen table with her milk and cookies, her mind racing as she devised the details of how she would proceed.

Chapter 5

The next afternoon Sarah called Tom to tell him what a great time she had the previous evening. They arranged for another date the next evening.

Everything happened very quickly over the next few weeks. Tom and Sarah saw each other almost every day; they went to movies, plays, concerts, sporting events, and dinners at most of the restaurants in town.

Sarah lavished attention and affection on Tom, who was clearly smitten with the beautiful young woman.

One evening in late spring, Sarah and Tom sat at a table on the veranda of the country club. They had eaten a late dinner and were just finished eating their Baked Alaska desserts.

"You seem kind of nervous tonight," Sarah observed.

"I'm just a nervous sort of guy."

"That's true, but you seem unusually jumpy this evening."

"I'm trying to decide when it's the right time."

"The right time for what?" she asked.

"For this." Tom got out of his chair, stooped down on one knee, and pulled a small box out of his jacket pocket. He opened the box to reveal a diamond ring. "Sarah, I love you. Will you marry me?"

Sarah had planned for this to happen, but she was still startled when the actual moment arrived. She was almost surprised by how genuinely pleased that she was by the proposal.

"Of course, Tom. I would love to be your wife." She held out her left hand so that he could slip the ring onto her finger.

As they kissed, several persons at nearby tables, having observed the proposal, applauded the newly-engaged couple.

Although Sarah wanted to get married as soon as possible, they found that they needed to wait several months in order to attend marriage preparation classes and to make preparations for the wedding and reception.

Tom was sympathetic to the difficulties with which Sarah's parents were dealing. He arranged for her father to get a management job at Angelique Plastiques. He also paid for Sarah's mother to receive some excellent, specialized medical treatments, and her mother's health soon showed clear improvement.

Early one Tuesday afternoon, Sarah drove her mother to the hospital and went to sit in the waiting room while her mother was being treated. The re-run of an old detective show was playing on the television mounted on the wall of the waiting room.

Sarah divided her attention between watching the television and observing the patients and hospital staff moving back and forth through the hallway. Then she spotted a little, blonde-haired girl pulling a wagon down the hall, and the television show was forgotten.

I have previously seen that girl somewhere, Sarah thought. I guess that it must have been here at the hospital when I brought my mother for one of her visits. No, it wasn't here. I'm sure of it. Where did I see her?

As the child passed by the glass wall of the waiting room, she turned and looked directly at Sarah, almost as though she knew that the young woman was thinking about her. The girl smiled pleasantly at Sarah, but did not pause as she continued her trek on some unknown mission. Sarah noted that there was a wisdom beyond her years in the child's eyes.

For several seconds, Sarah considered going after the child in order to speak with her. However, she then realized that she had no idea what she would say to the girl. Why are you so joyful? What do you know that I don't know?

Sarah's musings ended as her mother entered the waiting room; her treatment was finished, and she was ready to go home.

As they walked toward the exit, Sarah glanced down the hallway, but the girl has already passed out of sight.

During the month of May, Sarah was busy preparing for her wedding. She brought her mother and her friend, Kara, with her to help her make decisions. One day the three women went downtown to the bridal shop and selected a wedding dress for Sarah. The process was surprisingly easy as all three women agreed that one dress was clearly the best.

The next day they returned downtown in order to select dresses for the bridesmaids and to make arrangements with the florist and the photographer. Again, everything went smoothly.

In early June, the wedding day finally arrived. The weather was sunny as everyone gathered for the Mass at St. Faustina Church.

Many persons commented on what a gorgeous bride Sarah was.

Tom's sister, Nancy, was one of Sarah's bridesmaids. Kara was the maid-of-honor.

Tom saw Sarah in her wedding dress for the first time when she was escorted by her father down the main aisle.

"I am truly a fortunate man," he commented to his father, who was standing next to Tom. His father had been pleasantly surprised when Tom asked him to be the best man.

Because of Tom's background in theater and music, he had selected the songs for the ceremony as well as finding two excellent singers, a man and woman who were active in local theater groups.

During the ceremony, they sang as duets "The Servant Song", "How Beautiful is the Body of Christ", and "Come Gracious Spirit, Heavenly Dove". The woman and man also sang a couple of solos, and they later received many compliments on their excellent voices.

Father Kinsella officiated at the wedding and was the celebrant of the Mass.

In his homily, the priest emphasized that God needed to be an integral part of a successful marriage. "In his book,**Three to Get Married**, Fulton Sheen teaches us that God must be at the center of our lives because God is 'intrinsic to our nature, as blooming is to a flower. As trees in the forest bend through other trees to absorb the light, so every self is striving for the Love which is God.'"

Everyone in the congregation was impressed by Father Kinsella's warm, engaging manner.

The reception was held at the country club. Several men joked that they were going to sneak out onto the golf course to play a couple of holes, but no one actually did.

Late in the evening, Tom and Sarah slipped out of the reception and headed for the best hotel in town where they spent their wedding night. Early the next afternoon, the newlyweds drove north to the Wisconsin Dells vacation resort for their weeklong honeymoon.

CHAPTER 6

On a bright Saturday afternoon in mid-August, Tom and Sarah walked along Main Street downtown. They had been married for almost two months, and their new house was proving to be a lot of work. That afternoon they had made numerous purchases at a home warehouse store and at a lawn and garden store.

Some purchases they had managed to squeeze into the trunk of their car, but many larger items were going to be delivered during the week including a fountain and patio benches for their large backyard.

"Well, we accomplished quite a lot today," Sarah said as they walked along Main Street.

"Yes. It was a good day." He glanced at the time on his cell phone. "It's 4:30. Let's go over to St. Faustina's for 5 o'clock Mass."

"Okay, but it's a bit early to get there."

"They have confessions from 4 to 4:50. I haven't been to confession for a few months; I would like to go today."

"Tom, you are like a living saint. What could you possibly have to confess?"

Tom smiled. "That's between the priest and me. Besides, we receive grace each time we receive the sacrament of penance, so it's worthwhile going even we don't have much to confess."

"All right. I suppose that I might as well go to confession too since we're here," Sarah said as they approached the front steps of the church.

After going inside, they sat down in a pew a short distance from the confessional that was being used.

"Do you want to go first?" Tom asked upon seeing a person coming out of the confessional.

"Sure." She got up and left the pew.

Sarah entered the confessional and glanced at the kneeler by the screen where she could confess anonymously, but she decided to go around to the other side of the screen for a face-to-face confession.

"Hello, Father Kinsella." She sat down across from the priest.

"Hello Sarah. Good afternoon."

"It seems like I was just here a few weeks ago, but it has been almost eight months."

"Time passes swiftly," the priest agreed.

"My husband is going to come in here for his confession after I'm finished."

"I'm glad that you are both receiving the sacrament of penance today."

"As you might recall, when I made my last confession, I was very concerned about confidentiality. Can you guarantee that you won't tell my husband anything that I tell you?"

"I will not and cannot reveal anything about what you tell me to your husband or to anyone else."

"Good. I believe you."

"You can go ahead with your confession."

"I did not attend Mass on some Sundays. My husband often wanted me to go with him, so I usually went, but some weeks I just skipped Mass. I would tell Tom that I was going to a different Mass with my parents or one of my friends, but really I didn't go at all. Usually I would just go shopping.

"I have committed adultery numerous times in the past two months. My boyfriend from California now lives in this town, and we see each other at least once a week.

"I like Tom, but I mainly married him for his money. I might divorce him in another year or two. However, I need to stay in the marriage long enough for me to get a good divorce settlement.

"I'm actually happy with my life at the moment. Tom fulfills my social and financial needs, and my boyfriend fulfills my physical needs and adds excitement to my life."

She paused to study the priest's face, which remained impassive. "When I was here previously, you told me that very few things shock you since you hear so many confessions. You have to be at least a little shocked by what I just revealed to you."

"I'm not shocked, but I am concerned about the path that you are on. This adulterous affair and lack of commitment to your marriage can only end badly. The happiness that you presently feel is superficial and short-lived."

"Well, that's how things are, Father."

"I would recommend that you pray for at least a few minutes every day for God to give you the strength to end the affair and to fully commit to your marriage."

"I seem to almost have an addiction to my boyfriend. I can't imagine life without him, but I can imagine life without Tom."

"Give prayer a try, Sarah. You can pray anywhere, of course, but it is especially effective to pray in a church in the presence of the Blessed Sacrament. Our church is open every day of the week. You can stop by and sit here in the presence of Jesus Christ. Although the consecrated Host on the altar still resembles bread, the Host is now Jesus Christ as really present here as when he was born in Bethlehem and when he walked the hills of Galilee."

"I will try to pray, Father, and to come to Eucharistic adoration." Maybe I will, and maybe I won't, she thought.

"And as you go through your activities during the day, you can enter into a spiritual Communion by desiring the sacrament and by uniting your heart to the Heart of Jesus in the Eucharist. I have found spiritual Communion to be very helpful for my own spiritual growth."

"Yes, Father. I will do my best."

"Good. It's important that we keep trying to overcome sin. We all fail from time to time, but we need to try not to become discouraged. Discouragement is a tool of the devil."

"Yes, Father."

"If you have any additional sins, you can continue listing them, Sarah."

"That's everything, Father."

With his help, she recited the Act of Contrition prayer. He gave her absolution and instructed her to say the Our Father, Hail Mary, and Glory Be prayers every day that week.

After leaving the confessional, she walked over to the pew where Tom was seated.

"Your turn," she said as she sat down.

He was in the confessional for about three minutes. Sarah continually glanced over because she wanted to see his expression when he came out. She was certain that the priest would not directly tell him what she had revealed during her confession; however, she was concerned that something in the priest's manner might reveal to Tom that all was not well in his marriage. I should have let him go to confession first, she reprimanded herself.

To her relief, when he emerged from the confessional, he had a pleasant expression on his face. She knew that even though Tom was a skilled actor who could feign any emotion, he was not at all duplicitous. Father had not given away, either intentionally or unintentionally, the fact that there was a problem with their marriage.

On a Wednesday afternoon in August, Sarah and Kara met at the country club in order to play tennis.

During the warm months, the two women would play about once a week. They were both fairly good players, but neither was especially competitive; sometimes they did not even bother keeping score. Usually, though, they would warm up for a few minutes and then play one set.

Today Kara was the better player. She served several aces and was getting in most of her first serves. Sarah served many double faults and seemed distracted.

While leading 5 games to 1, Kara glided gracefully across the court and hit a perfect backhand down the line. Sarah dashed toward it, but she could not reach the ball in time.

"Nice shot!" Sarah declared. "That's game, set, and match!"

"Thanks!" Kara grinned. "Let's get some lunch!"

As the two attractive women, blonde and brunette, walked through the patio restaurant, they drew many admiring glances.

They selected a table with a good view and ordered salads and sodas.

"Are you and Tom going on a trip this summer?" Kara asked.

"I'm not sure. We might go to the Wisconsin Dells again for a few days. The waterparks there are great, and Tom likes the golf course, and I enjoy the spa there."

"The Dells are a lot of fun, but you went there for your honeymoon. Why don't you go someplace else? You should go to Florida or Hawaii!"

"Oh, I guess that I never told you about Tom's inner ear problem. He can't fly because he gets severe vertigo that lasts for a day or two after he gets off the plane."

"I see. I didn't know. Well, you and Tom could drive to Florida or to California. If you drive to the West Coast, you could then take a cruise ship to Hawaii. Or, if you drive to the East Coast, you could take a cruise to Bermuda or the Caribbean islands."

Sarah laughed. "Tom and I recently talked about some similar ideas! You must have our house bugged!"

"I do," Kara giggled. "And the things that I hear! You are a very naughty girl!"

"You are right about me being naughty, but you wouldn't find that out by eavesdropping on me at home."

"Do tell!"

Sarah hesitated. For the past couple of weeks, she had been considering telling Kara about the affair with Wayne. She wanted Kara's advice. Kara was her best friend, and Sarah trusted Kara to keep her secret. However, unlike a priest, Kara was not bound by the seal of confession; with her friend, there was no certainty that the secret would be kept forever. A priest would take her secrets with him to his grave.

"Come on, Sarah, what's up!" Kara prodded her.

Sarah shook her head. "Nothing. I was just being silly."

"You didn't seem to be able to concentrate on our tennis game today. I can tell that something is worrying you."

"I get frustrated with Tom sometimes. Besides his inner ear problem, he is allergic to dust, dogs, cats, most types of flowers, and many types of food. There are some restaurants where we never eat because Tom is allergic to almost everything on the menu."

"We all have our weaknesses and limitations, Sarah. I also have cat and dust allergies, and I'm allergic to penicillin. And I have a lot of idiosyncrasies: I hate candles because I'm afraid that they will start a fire; I don't like gum, and it annoys me when someone chews gum around me. That is just the tip of the iceberg."

"But you can fly in an airplane."

"And I can eat in any restaurant in town," Kara said. "You can go with me to all those restaurants where Tom can't eat the food. I will even let you treat!"

Sarah grinned. "That's a good idea, but I think that Dutch treat at those restaurants is an even better idea."

"Let's play it by ear," Kara chuckled.

"I just had another idea. I haven't been back to California since I graduated from college. I would love to go back there to go to the beaches and visit some friends. I don't want to drive all the way there with Tom, though. How about flying with me to California for a few days? I will pay for your plane ticket and for our hotel room."

"That sounds great. Will it be okay with Tom?"

"Yeah, it will be fine with him. In fact, last week he suggested that I take my parents on a trip."

"Hmmm. It sounds like he wants to get you out of town for a few days. He might have found himself a girlfriend. You'd better keep an eye on him."

"Perhaps he'd better keep a closer eye on me." Sarah instantly regretted making this statement.

"What does that mean?"

"I'm just kidding."

Kara looked at her with wide eyes. "Sarah, are you having an affair?" she asked in a whisper.

"I have been faithful in my heart," Sarah said in a low voice.

"You are having an affair! Who is he?"

"During my last two years of college, I had a boyfriend named Wayne Kirchner. He followed me back here. We were sleeping together in California and continued to do so here, even after I got married."

"I would never have guessed. Don't you love Tom?"

"I don't know. Probably. I suppose so, but Wayne is more exciting. I have often resolved to break up with Wayne; however, I always relent and go back to him."

"You seem to be addicted to him," Kara said.

"I feel that my relationship with Wayne is more of a habit than an addiction—a bad habit. Perhaps doing some traveling would be helpful because it would keep me away from Wayne. If I don't see him so much, I might be able to break that habit."

"It's worth a try. When do we leave for California?"

Sarah laughed. "It certainly didn't take much persuading to get you to go with me."

"If you're paying for the trip, I'll go with you to Europe, Australia, Hawaii, or anywhere you want."

"But don't you have to arrange at your job to take time off from work?" Sarah asked.

"That won't be a problem. Summer is a slow time at work. In fact, they prefer for us to use our vacation time in the summer."

"Okay, then let's fly to Los Angeles next week," Sarah said. "We can rent a car there. I'll show you all the hot spots in Southern California!"

"Great! I'm sure that we'll have a wonderful time!"

CHAPTER 7

Exactly a week later, Sarah and Kara were relaxing on beach towels as they worked on their suntans on Santa Monica beach. The next day they visited a couple of other beaches and did some snorkeling.

The two women then drove to San Diego for dinner and some shopping.

Kara had never been to Disneyland, so the next morning they went to Anaheim and spent the entire day in Disneyland.

The trip went so well that they looked forward to traveling together again sometime soon and discussed several possibilities for their next trip.

In early September, Tom and Sarah drove to Chicago for a short vacation. On Friday they spent most of the day at Navy Pier. They went for a two-hour cruise on the Tall Ship Windy. Both Tom and Sarah were among the passengers who helped the crew raise the sails, and they each had a turn taking the wheel and steering the ship for a few minutes.

Upon returning to the pier, they visited many of the shops. In a shop specializing in Russian products, Sarah purchased a large

Matryoshka nesting doll which contained progressively smaller dolls depicting characters from a classic Russian fairy tale.

They ventured into the mall's maze that included a hall of mirrors.

"This is like something that you would find in Hogwarts Castle in a Harry Potter novel!" Sarah laughed uproariously as they tried to find their way out of the maze.

A short distance from the maze, Tom was especially glad to see a 500-seat theater that featured Shakespeare plays. Later they enjoyed strolling through Navy Pier's museum of stained glass windows and exploring the Crystal Gardens, a one-acre botanical gardens.

"I could spend a week at Navy Pier!" Sarah declared enthusiastically.

In the evening they walked along the Magnificent Mile on Michigan Avenue. Sarah took numerous photos of the thousands of tulips and other colorful flowers that lined the sidewalks for almost the entire mile.

On Saturday they went to the Shedd Aquarium, the Chicago Art Institute, and to the top of the Hancock Tower. On Sunday Tom and Sarah attended a morning Mass at the Holy Name Cathedral, then took a cab to the Lincoln Park Zoo.

It was a good trip, and they planned to make another trip to Chicago again sometime in the near future.

"With all those wonderful stores along the Magnificent Mile and at Navy Pier, I could get all of my Christmas shopping done in Chicago!" Sarah said as they drove back home.

In late September, Sarah took her parents on a cruise to Bermuda. It was the first time that any of them had been on a cruise ship. Sarah's parents enjoyed many of the onboard activities including the musical shows and the classes on various activities.

Her father was pleased that golf lessons were offered. He had begun to play golf occasionally at the country club and was always looking for tips to improve his game.

Her mother attended some spinning classes in which the students rode stationary bicycles while the instructor at the front of the class would encourage the students as they made an imaginary journey through various types of terrain.

Sarah took several scuba diving lessons during the cruise. The first couple of classes were held in the ship's pool. When the ship arrived in Bermuda, the class moved onto the beach, and the students were allowed to venture into the Atlantic Ocean. Sarah was fascinated with exploring the undersea world and loved seeing the many colorful species of fish.

Whenever Sarah departed on a trip, Wayne immediately drove to Chicago or Milwaukee. He had begun doing some casual drug dealing, mainly with persons that he met in nightclubs.

Eventually, a major heroin dealer in Chicago offered him a lucrative deal which involved Wayne distributing drugs to many small towns in northern Illinois and Wisconsin. Because of the dangers presented by the police and by violent criminals, Wayne initially was reluctant to accept the deal. However, the money was so good that he decided to try it for a while.

Wayne was glad that he had a Glock pistol that he had stolen from the intoxicated man in Sarah's hometown. Wayne purchased a bulletproof vest, but he found the vest uncomfortable and only wore it when he was meeting someone for a drug deal.

He liked the Glock pistol, though, and almost everywhere that he went, he wore the pistol in a shoulder holster concealed beneath his jacket.

Wayne was fascinated by the gun's fine engineering and sleek appearance. The pistol was the perfect weight and felt good in his hand.

One Saturday evening, while Sarah was thousands of miles away on a cruise with her parents, Wayne drove from Chicago to a small industrial town about sixty miles northwest of the city. He was scheduled to meet with a new customer there.

Shortly after dusk, he drove slowly through the town's warehouse district as he scanned the street signs. Eventually he spotted a warehouse located at the address for which he had been searching. Wayne turned into the parking lot.

There was only one other car in the lot. A tall, thin man in his twenties was leaning against the car as he smoked a cigarette. He had an unpleasant expression.

Wayne frowned as he noted the beat-up car and sleazy-looking man. I don't like the way that this looks, Wayne thought as he opened his jacket and made sure that the holstered gun was within easy reach.

He parked about thirty feet away from the man's car and got out.

"Hey, what's up?" Wayne said casually, taking a couple of steps toward the man.

"Not much." The man tossed aside his cigarette. "Are you Wayne?"

"Yeah. I have your merchandise. Do you have the money?"

"Yes." He reached through the open window of his car and pulled out a duffel bag that he held in front of him. "Let's see the merchandise."

"Okay." Wayne went back to his car, opened the trunk, and took out a briefcase. After closing the trunk, he walked toward the man. "This is good quality stuff. I'm sure that you will be pleased."

Wayne noticed the man's eyes move past him as though he were looking at something or someone behind him.

Wayne half-turned, following the man's glance. There was a second man standing in the darkened doorway of the factory.

"Who is he?" Wayne asked, becoming nervous.

"He is just a guy who works with me. You don't need to worry about him. He's just here to make sure that everything is cool."

"Are you cops?"

"No, man. Come on. Let's see the merchandise!"

"I don't like having somebody behind me," Wayne said. "Have him come over here, and I'll show you both the merchandise at the same time."

"Come here," the man called to his friend, waving him forward.

As the other man approached, Wayne took a step backward so that he could better watch both men. Wayne observed that this second man had the same mean-spirited expression as his friend. He wondered whether they were brothers.

Wayne snapped open the briefcase that was packed with heroin. "Here it is." After giving them a few seconds to get a clear look at the contents, Wayne snapped the briefcase shut and handed it to the first man.

Wayne pointed at the duffel bag. "Now I will take your payment and be on my way."

"The money is all here. You can count it if you want." The first man tried to hand Wayne the duffel bag.

"Would you unzip the bag and hold it open for me please?" Wayne asked.

"Here it is, man. Count the money yourself."

Wayne did not like doing it this way, but he was anxious to complete the transaction. He reluctantly allowed the man to give him the duffel bag. While unzipping it, he continually glanced up at both men.

The bag contained a few bundles of small denomination bills on top of some newspapers. Wayne instantly knew the attack was coming.

The second, smaller man had been concealing a switchblade knife at his side. He lunged at Wayne, the blade of the knife puncturing Wayne's shirt and cutting into the bulletproof vest, but not penetrating it.

Wayne staggered backward, throwing the duffel bag at the men to distract them for a moment.

As he reached for the Glock pistol in his shoulder holster, he saw that the first, taller man was also drawing a gun from his pocket. Wayne was a bit faster, though. His first shot went through the man's chest, and his second shot went through the forehead.

The second man with the knife was stepping forward with the blade raised for an overhead strike, but Wayne saw him coming and fired wildly. The bullet hit the man in the left thigh, causing him to drop the knife. He fell to his right knee, clutching the wounded left thigh.

Realizing that he was out of danger, Wayne's racing heartbeat began to slow down. He looked at the wounded man, trying to decide what to do with him.

The man looked up at Wayne. "Please don't kill me."

Wayne said nothing and glared at the man.

"Mercy," the man pleaded.

"Mercy. Now that's an interesting concept. You and your friend planned to rob and kill me, and now you want me to be merciful."

"Don't shoot me. Mercy."

"It would be bad for business to allow you to live. I need to make an example of you."

Wayne fired one shot into his head, and the man collapsed dead onto the parking lot. *Well, at least I put you out of your pain from the thigh wound,* Wayne thought with grim humor. *I guess this could be considered a mercy killing.*

Wayne picked up the duffel bag. It contained an insignificant amount of money, but his fingerprints were on the bag, so he needed to take it with him.

He retrieved his briefcase containing the heroin, then hurried back to his car. Although it was a fairly isolated area, Wayne realized that someone might have heard the gunshots and called the police. He needed to get away as quickly as possible.

Wayne drove off the parking lot and headed down the street leading to the highway. *Mercy,* he recalled the man's last word. *That is something which would appeal to Sarah. It's too bad for that guy that she wasn't the one holding the gun to his head. He would still be alive tomorrow.*

This drug business is too damned dangerous, he reflected. *I almost got killed tonight. If I do this long enough, my luck is* eventually going to run out. I'm only going to do this for another month or two. I need to find a safer way to get a lot of money. Sarah. She's the way for me to get rich. All we need to do is kill her husband and then we'll be millionaires.

As Wayne pulled onto the highway access ramp, the two dead men back on the parking lot were already forgotten. He was thinking about what he would say to Sarah the next time that he saw her, how he would manipulate her into going along with his plan.

CHAPTER 8

Just a few hours after Sarah returned home from the weeklong cruise with her parents, she received a call on her cell phone from Wayne. He wanted her to come to his apartment.

"Wayne, I'm too tired. We had a long flight to Chicago and then a long drive home."

"Okay, baby, I understand. Come to see me tomorrow, though."

She reluctantly agreed. However, the next day, when Sarah had still not arrived by early evening, Wayne called her again and cajoled her into coming over.

Two hours later, after getting out of the bed in his apartment, Sarah and Wayne poured themselves drinks and sat on the couch. They watched television for a while, but soon became bored and turned the television off.

"Hey, baby, I want to talk to you about something."

"What?"

"Now I want you to listen to my whole idea before you shoot it down."

"No, you cannot run any scams here in my hometown," she said, anticipating what he was going to say.

"That's not what I want to talk about. A couple of days ago I was talking on the phone to a lawyer friend of mine, and without giving your names, I described your situation with your husband."

"That situation is fine." Sarah was annoyed. "Don't be talking about me to any lawyers."

"Listen, what he said is important. You are planning to file for divorce next year, but you aren't going to get anywhere near as much money in the settlement as you think that you are. There is no way that you are going to get half of his money and possessions. You will have only been married less than two years; there are no children; and he already had almost all of that wealth before he married you."

"I will still get a very large alimony check every month."

"Yeah, probably, but why settle for that when you can have so much more."

"What do you mean?"

"Your little hubby could have a fatal accident. You would inherit everything as well as collect on his life insurance policies."

"I'm not killing my husband, you psycho."

"It would be the perfect solution. Instead of waiting until next year, you could be free from him in a few weeks. No messy divorce, no lawyers. And you would be an instant multi-millionaire."

"No."

"We would make it look like an accident. There are a dozen different ways that we could do it. Maybe just knock him out with a roofie, put him in the driver's seat in his car, and send it over a cliff."

"I won't do it, and I won't allow you to do it."

"Why not?" He paused and then added with a sly expression, "It's not like he would be the first person that you have killed."

She looked at him intently. "What do you mean?"

"Just forget that I said that, baby. I don't want upset you. Let's have another drink."

"Damn it! I have never killed anyone! What are you talking about?"

"Do you remember Bruce, the insurance salesman who was attending a convention in Las Vegas?"

"Yes. We met him in a casino bar. While his attention was focused on me, you slipped him a roofie. He passed out in the hallway outside of his hotel room, and I took the money out of his wallet. It was no big deal. I'm sure that he was fine when he woke up."

"Actually, he wasn't fine. In fact, he died. He had some medical problems, and he had a seizure as a result of the drug that we gave him."

"You're lying!"

He walked over to his suitcase that was in a corner of the bedroom. He reached inside an inner pocket in the suitcase and removed a cut-out newspaper article.

"You really should read the newspaper every day, Sarah. You would be much better informed about what is going on in the world."

"Just give me that." She snatched the article from him and began reading.

The article reported that a 56-year-old insurance salesman named Bruce Englemann had been found dead in a hotel hallway. His death was considered suspicious and an autopsy was going to be performed. The article mentioned that Bruce had epilepsy and a mild heart condition. He was married with two children who were in college.

"No!" She shouted, throwing the article away from her. "This must be about some other guy. The Bruce that I met was fine when I left him."

"I'm sorry that this upset you so much, baby, but you know that this is the same guy. All of the details match up perfectly with the guy that we scammed—same date, same name, same place. Everything is the same."

"This article is from over a year ago. Why didn't you show this to me before now?"

"I didn't want to upset you, baby. I know what a kind heart you have."

"You put the drug into his drink! You are the one who killed him! All that I did was talk to him!"

"We were working as a team, baby. It doesn't matter which of us actually gave him the roofie. We are both responsible for what happened."

She began weeping. He pretended to console her, all the while trying to determine how long he should wait until he again brought up the subject of eliminating her husband.

Two weeks later Sarah went into the confessional. She walked over to the chair and sat down.

"Hello, Sarah. It's certainly nice and warm outside today."

"Yes, Father. I was playing tennis earlier this afternoon."

"It's been over a year since I played tennis. I need to get back out there on the court before my game gets too rusty."

"You are always welcome to play at the country club as my guest, Father."

"Thank you, Sarah. I'll stop by out there sometime."

"I hope that you will still want to be my guest there after you hear my confession."

"We are all sinners, Sarah. Only Jesus and His mother are without sin, Sarah. In this life, we are pilgrims on a journey."

"I must be a very wicked pilgrim."

"You can go ahead with your confession, Sarah."

"Bless me, Father, for I have sinned. It has been about one month since my last confession. During this period, I again committed some of the same sins that I have previously confessed. I failed to attend Mass on two Sundays, and I committed adultery five times. In addition, I recently learned that I accidentally killed someone last year."

"How did this person's death occur?"

"Father, as you might recall from one of my previous confessions, my boyfriend and I used to work a scam where we would slip a drug into a person's drink and later rob the person. I recently learned that one man died several hours after Wayne gave him the drug. I distracted the man while Wayne slipped a pill into his drink. Apparently, the man had epilepsy and heart problems, and he had such a bad reaction to the drug that he died. I feel terrible that this happened. I have been crying about it all week."

"Well, since you didn't intend to kill or permanently hurt this person, that reduces your moral culpability. And you didn't personally place the drug into the man's drink. However, you were aware that there was a risk of someone dying after being give one of those drugs, so you must bear some responsibility. I have previously granted you absolution for these incidents, but it is good that you have let me know about this new aspect of this earlier sin. I can grant you absolution today for your indirect participation in this person's death."

"That's good, Father. The man with whom I am having the affair just informed me a week ago about the death. He has known about it for over a year, and he even has the newspaper story. However, last week he decided to finally tell me about it."

"Why did he finally decide to tell you about it?"

"He thought that he could use that news to manipulate me into doing something that I am reluctant to do."

"I'm glad that you realize that this man is manipulating you."

"Yes. I'm smarter than he thinks that I am. He believes that if I realize that I have already participated in killing one person, I will be more willing to kill a second person. To his warped way of thinking, once you are already a murderer, it doesn't matter that much whether you kill one person or ten persons."

"What does he want you to do?"

"He wants me to murder my husband. He says that we can arrange to make Tom's death look like an accident."

"I hope that you are not considering committing this murder."

"No. I would never intentionally kill Tom or anyone else."

"Good."

"Even if I was not arrested, I know that I would regret it for the rest of my life."

"Do you think that there is a possibility that this man might act on his own to try to kill Tom?"

"I doubt it, but I will talk to him. I'll tell him that I will turn him in to the police if anything happens to Tom."

"This man is very dangerous. You need to be very careful."

"I know, Father."

"And you need to continue to pray for the strength to stop seeing this man. Even if you were a single woman, it would be necessary for you to get away from him. He is on a road toward destruction, and he is taking you with him along that road."

"Yes, Father."

After the priest said the words of absolution, Sarah thanked him and said good-bye.

CHAPTER 9

Sarah was glad when she did not hear from Wayne for several days. She assumed that he was in Chicago; he was spending increasing amounts of time there recently. I suppose that this small town bores him, Sarah reflected. He likes the big city with all its nightclubs. He probably has one or two girlfriends in Chicago and is sleeping with them. She realized with some surprise that she did not care whether Wayne had relationships with other women.

Late one afternoon Wayne called Sarah on her cell phone. They arranged to meet at their favorite pub at eight o'clock that evening.

When she entered the pub, there were only a handful of persons inside. Sarah did not see Wayne and walked over to the bar to wait for him. She started to sit down on a stool when she heard his familiar voice.

"Hey, baby, over here!" Wayne called to her from a booth in the corner.

"Oh, hey." She walked toward him. "I didn't see you there." As she got closer to him, she frowned. She looked with distaste at his thin mustache. "I might not have recognized you even if I had seen you. What is the deal with the mustache?"

"I decided to change my style. I need to look cool when I go to the nightclubs in Chicago."

She sat down next to him in the booth. Some men looked good with a mustache, and some men did not. Wayne was definitely in the latter category, Sarah thought.

"One of the few good things about you Wayne is that you are handsome. That mustache hurts your looks."

He laughed. "Is that so?"

"Take my advice: lose the mustache."

"I'm going to keep it for a while."

"Suit yourself."

"You are looking hot this evening, baby. I like the short skirt and high heels. Everyone in this place was checking you out when you were over by the bar."

"Thanks. So how did everything go in Chicago?"

"Really good. I am expanding my horizons."

"What does that mean?"

"I've been making some useful contacts lately, both in Chicago and Milwaukee. I should be able to make a lot of money. Maybe one day I'll be as rich as your little husband."

"What scam are you working now?"

"Those scams have been profitable, and they were fun for a while, but they are starting to get boring. I'm a businessman now. I have a franchise to distribute China white in this area."

"China white!" Sarah was so shocked that she just barely remembered to keep her voice down. "China white is heroin! Are you a heroin dealer now?"

"Easy, baby. It's all good. You've used China white yourself. Why are you getting so self-righteous?"

"I tried a very small amount once at a party at Berkley. I didn't like it."

"Well, a lot of people do like it. I'm providing them with what they want."

"Have you forgotten that a girl in my dorm died from using heroin?" Sarah asked.

"She was doing speedballs combining heroin with cocaine," Wayne said. "It was a stupid thing to do. The cocaine causes the heartbeat to speed up, and the heroin causes the heartbeat to slow down. When you combine the two drugs, the heart can get all out of sync and never recover the correct rhythm. Lots of people have died from doing speedballs."

Sarah stared at him. "So you are going to help persons kill themselves?"

"I'm not selling them cocaine, just heroin. And I'm only selling them the heroin, not injecting it into them. They are adults and are responsible for their own actions."

"Is there anything that you do that you can't rationalize?"

"Give me a break! You didn't used to be this self-righteous. Besides using heroin that time, you did cocaine at least a half-dozen times back in California. I know because I did the cocaine with you. And we got drunk almost every weekend."

"I have made plenty of mistakes. Well, I now understand your new look better. You look like a drug dealer because you are a drug dealer."

"I'm actually more involved with the distribution end of the business. When a China white shipment arrives in Chicago, I go there and pick up the product. Then I drive to a number of towns in northern Illinois and southern Wisconsin to drop off the product to the dealers."

"This is a big mistake, Wayne. You should get out before you get in too deep."

"I don't want to get out."

"You are going to end up either dead or in prison for many years."

"Only if I get stupid or careless."

"Everybody makes careless mistakes from time to time."

"Not me."

"And getting involved with drugs shows that you are stupid."

"Man, baby, there you go again! You are as cold as they come. This town really knew what it was doing when it made you the Ice Princess!"

"Yeah, and they liked me so much that they also made me the Snow Maiden."

"Snow Maiden, Ice Princess, who gives a damn? Now listen, baby, I want to talk about something important. Have you been considering what I suggested the last time that I saw you?"

"To which of your suggestions are you referring?" Sarah asked, but she knew what he wanted to discuss.

"About arranging for the accidental death of your husband."

"I told you that I would not consider doing such a thing."

"You should consider it. We could make it look like a car accident. There would be no chance of us getting caught."

"No."

"This would be the perfect scam. We would both be millionaires."

"I am already a millionaire."

"After you divorce him, you might not be a millionaire any longer."

"I'm not sure whether I want to divorce him."

Wayne stared at her. "What?"

"You heard me."

"You have got to be kidding me! You want to spend the rest of your life with that guy?"

"I'm considering it."

"Unbelievable. You have changed, Sarah."

"Yes. For the better, I hope."

"That's not the way that I see it."

"I don't have much time this evening. I'd better get going."

"Listen, baby, wait. I wasn't going to tell you this because I didn't want to worry you."

"Tell me what?"

"You are actually right about the dangers of dealing drugs. About a month ago, I almost got killed when I took a China white shipment to some town near Chicago. Two guys ambushed me in the parking lot of a warehouse. I got into a shootout with them, and I was able to get away. If I hadn't been wearing my bulletproof vest, I would have been killed."

"Good grief, Wayne! Why didn't you tell me about this before now?"

"I told you, baby; I didn't want you to worry about me."

"What happened to the two men who attacked you?"

"I got off a few shots with my Glock pistol. It's a great gun! I killed both of them."

"Good Lord, Wayne, the police are probably after you!"

"It was self-defense. They were trying to kill me. I have a right to defend myself."

"I'm not sure whether pleading self-defense will work when persons are killed in a drug deal gone bad."

"It doesn't matter. The police have no idea that I did it. And I won't ever make another delivery to that town. But this drug dealing is dangerous, and I'm going to have to keep doing it unless you help me out. If your husband dies in an accident, I won't have to sell drugs anymore. And no more scams. His death will be our last scam and greatest scam."

"You already have a lot of money from all those scams in California and Las Vegas. And I'm sure that your drug dealing has been quite profitable for you. Be content with what you have."

"I'm a high roller, baby. You're right that I have a lot of cash, but I want millions."

"Then find some other way to make your millions. I'm not harming my husband."

"So you'd rather that I get shot by some drug dealers? That is what is going to happen sooner or later in this business."

"Did you ever study logic in any of your college classes? Your arguments are ridiculous!"

"Just continue to consider my suggestion about your husband."

Sarah stood up, picking up her purse. "I'm tired, Wayne. I'm going to call it a night and head home."

He rose from the seat and kissed her on the cheek. "Okay, baby. I'm going to get another drink before I leave. Think about what I said. I'll call you tomorrow."

"Good night, Wayne."

As Sarah departed from the bar, she made the decision to end this relationship with Wayne. However, when he called her again about a week later, she went to his apartment and stayed there for about an hour and a half.

CHAPTER 10

The world was ice. At least it seemed so to Tom as he walked hurriedly across the wind-swept parking lot and through the plaza of Angelique Plastiques. It had sleeted the previous night and now strong winds took the wind-chill factor to far below zero. Tom was glad as the sliding automatic doors parted, and he entered the warmth of the lobby.

Tom exchanged "good mornings" with the receptionist and security guard, then took the elevator up to the corporate offices. As he stepped out of the elevator, it almost seemed as if he had been magically transported into a tropical garden.

The reception area was filled with plants and even had a small waterfall that cascaded down into a pond. There was a small bridge over the pond in which several colorful Koi fish were swimming.

"It's always so nice in here," Tom said to his secretary.

"Yes, it is very peaceful," Rosemary replied. "When I eat lunch, I sometimes like to sit on the bench by the waterfall. It's kind of like a mini-picnic."

Tom laughed. "That sounds like a good idea. I'll have to try it myself sometime."

"Tom, your sister told me that she wanted to see you when you got in," Rosemary said.

"Am I in hot water?"

"That would be better than being in cold water on a day like this," Rosemary quipped.

"Ha! You have a point there."

"Seriously, Tom, she seemed to be in a good mood, so I don't think that you have anything to worry about."

"Good."

Tom walked down the hallway and leaned into the open doorway of his sister's office. Nancy was eight years older than Tom, and she had become the company's Chief Executive Officer last year after the retirement of their father.

"Knock, knock."

"Hi, Tom," Nancy said, looking up from some papers.

"What's up?"

"I finished reading your proposal to increase our company's charitable activities. You make some good points, Tom. Since we are an entirely family-owned company, we can do whatever we want with our profits. I like the idea of contributing some of our profits to faith-based organizations like the St. Vincent de Paul Society, Catholic Charities, the Eternal Word Television Network, the Legion of Christ, and the Society for the Propagation of the Faith."

Nancy glanced down at the sheet of paper that listed the charitable causes that he had recommended. "Let's see what else we have on here—Missionaries of the Poor, Missionaries of Charity, Passionist missions, Sacred Heart Southern Missions, Missionary Oblates of Mary Immaculate, … Hmmm, there seems to be a common theme here. This list could be a bit more ecumenical."

Tom laughed. "I do have the Salvation Army, Food for the Poor, and a few other ecumenical organizations on the list."

"I'm just kidding you. This is a great list. I can generally support the proposal, although we might have to scale back some of the contributions."

"Hopefully not scaled back too much."

Nancy chuckled. "We'll see. Even though Dad is retired, he is still the majority stockholder, and I need to present your proposal to him for his yea or nay. I like your idea about contacting faith-based charities in areas where we have factories. I'm sure that they would welcome our help. Many poor and homeless persons could be trained for good jobs with our company."

"I'm sure that Dad will be enthusiastic about our program, Nancy."

"Yeah, I'm sure that he will."

Rosemary appeared in the doorway. "Nancy and Tom, I'm sorry to interrupt. Tom, there is a gentleman waiting in the reception area who would like to see you. He doesn't have an appointment. I'm guessing that he is a salesman. Would you like me to tell him to come back some other time?"

"No, that's okay. I will talk to him."

"Do you want to meet me for lunch down in the cafeteria about noon?" Nancy asked as he walked out of her office.

"Yeah. I'll see you in the cafeteria at noon. I think that they are serving chili today."

"Good!"

Tom followed Rosemary back to the reception area where he saw the tall, middle-aged man waiting for him.

"Hello, I'm Tom Angelique," he said, shaking hands with the man.

"Very glad to meet you, Mr. Angelique. My name is Robert Alma."

"What can I do for you, Mr. Alma?"

"Perhaps we could speak in your office. This is a rather sensitive matter."

"Okay." Tom glanced over at Rosemary, who had just returned to her desk.

Rosemary shrugged, equally puzzled about what this man wanted.

Robert and Tom went into the office, and Tom shut the door.

"Have a seat," Tom said, gesturing toward the chair in front of his desk. After sitting down himself, he continued, "All right, you have the floor, Mr. Alma."

"Thank you. I'm a private investigator from Chicago. Last Friday evening my client was in a popular nightclub in Chicago when his wallet and briefcase were stolen by a man who befriended him. The briefcase contained some very sensitive documents that could cause a great deal of harm if they were made public.

"My client contacted me on Saturday morning, and we began trying to track down the thief. The thief's name is Wayne Kirchner. In recent months, he has been a frequent visitor to the most popular clubs in Chicago. Late on Saturday night, I spotted him leaving a nightclub and followed him to his hotel.

"For reasons that you would not want to know, I could not contact the police about this matter. I planned to break into his hotel room on Sunday in order to try to retrieve the briefcase and its valuable contents. However, Kirchner checked out early on Sunday morning before I had a chance to make my move."

"This is all very interesting, Mr. Alma, but what does it have to do with me?"

"Please be patient with me, Mr. Angelique. I promise that you will understand in just a few moments."

"Good. I was beginning to think that you had wandered into the wrong office."

"I'm afraid that you are going to wish that I did come to the wrong office. You aren't going to like the rest of my report."

"Please continue."

"Kirchner drove from Chicago to this town. I was able to follow him without him noticing me. I followed him to his apartment building, which is downtown. I got myself a motel room just a couple of blocks from his apartment.

"On Sunday afternoon and evening, I kept his apartment under close surveillance. If he had left the apartment, I would have tried to break in to retrieve the briefcase."

"Should you be telling me this? Breaking and entry is not legal."

"No, it's not. However, I never got the chance to break in because he did not leave the apartment. Several persons went in and out of the apartment building, and I kept a close watch to see whether he had passed the briefcase onto someone else. No one left the building with the briefcase, but I still photographed everyone who went in or out." He reached into the inner pocket of his jacket and pulled out a couple of photos, which he placed on the desk. "I believe that this lady is your wife, Sarah. She entered the apartment building at 7:35 p.m. and departed at 8:52 p.m."

Tom glanced down at the photos and picked up one. "Yes. This is Sarah. What are you implying, Mr. Alma?"

"I think that your wife was visiting Wayne Kirchner that evening."

"How large is this apartment building?"

"There are sixteen units in the building."

"Then she could have been visiting someone in one of those fifteen other apartments. Sarah grew up in this town, and she has many friends here. I would assume that she was visiting one of her female friends."

"That's possible, but it's more likely that she was visiting Kirchner. I have run background checks on both Kirchner and your wife. They attended the same college in California, and they graduated on the same day."

"It's a big university, Mr. Alma," Tom objected, but he experienced a sinking feeling. Although his mind raced seeking other explanations, he believed that the private detective had correctly assessed the situation.

"My wife would not associate with a criminal, and she would not be unfaithful to me."

"I have never met your wife, Mr. Angelique. I'm sorry if I have caused you any consternation. I'm sure that she is a fine young lady. Perhaps she doesn't know that this man is a criminal. And I don't know for certain that she is having an affair with him."

"She might have just gone to visit an old college friend who for some reason has moved to this town," Tom said without conviction.

"Frankly, the reason that I came here today is that I am hoping that you will hire me to get to the bottom of this business. I am a good private investigator, and I can assure you that I am very discreet. I will just give you all of the information that I obtain, and you can do with that information whatever you wish."

"You want me to hire you to follow my wife?"

"Basically, yes. I can work for two clients at the same time. Since I am here to retrieve that briefcase, I will have Kirchner and his apartment under surveillance. I can probably determine whether or not your wife is intimately involved with him."

Tom could feel his heart beating rapidly. If Sarah was involved with another man, that would explain a lot. Occasionally she would disappear for several hours, then reappear giving an implausible explanation about running an errand. After these incidents, Sarah would become emotionally withdrawn and distant for the rest of the day. The next morning, she would again be cheerful and talkative.

"Mr. Angelique?" the detective asked, taking Tom out of his thoughts and back to the present moment.

"Oh, I'm sorry. You have given me a lot to think about, Mr. Alma."

"I understand."

"To tell you the truth, I am concerned about what you have told me. However, I would not feel right about hiring a private detective to follow my wife. I will look into this situation myself." Tom pulled out his wallet and took out two hundred dollars, which he handed to Robert. "This payment is for your effort in coming here today and for giving me your report. I appreciate the information. I realize that I need to begin focusing more attention on my marriage."

"Thank you, Mr. Angelique." Robert stood and handed Tom his business card. "If I can be of future service on this matter or any other matter where a good private investigator would be helpful, just give me a call."

"I will do that." Tom placed the business card in his wallet. "Thanks for your help."

After the two men shook hands, they said good-bye and Robert departed.

Tom sat back down, staring at the wall, wondering what to do now.

CHAPTER 11

Many hours later, just after dark, Robert sat at a window booth in a diner from which he had a clear view of Wayne's apartment building. Robert was having his third cup of coffee as he waited for Wayne to appear. That guy sure spends a lot of time in his apartment, Robert reflected. What is he doing in there for all those hours? I suppose that he is doped up on some of those drugs that he has been buying recently.

If he would just go out for a half-hour or so, I could break into the apartment, grab the briefcase, and be on my way back to Chicago.

Sarah has not visited him today. I wonder whether Tom will say something to her this evening.

Robert's reflections were abruptly interrupted by the sudden emergence of Wayne from the building. He was carrying the briefcase.

Robert placed a tip on the table, then went hurrying out the front door of the diner. He spotted Wayne walking casually down a side street.

Why does he have the briefcase with him? Perhaps he has found someone to purchase its contents and is now on the way to make the sale, Robert thought.

Wayne walked through a small park and then across some railroad tracks. Robert followed him, keeping a safe distance back in order to remain unnoticed.

However, Wayne never glanced back and seemed completely unconcerned that someone might follow him. He went into a wooded area on the opposite side of the train tracks.

That must be where he is meeting the buyer, Robert thought, quickening his step as he lost sight of Wayne who was now in the dark woods.

As Robert crossed the tracks and moved into the woods, he realized that it would be prudent to be cautious. He pulled his pistol from the shoulder holster beneath his jacket.

Where is he? Robert moved further into the woods, but he could not see Wayne anywhere. Seeing a small bridge up ahead, he headed in that direction.

"Looking for somebody?" Wayne said, stepping out from behind the tree that Robert had just walked past. "Drop your gun and turn around slowly."

Robert mentally kicked himself for walking into a trap.

"I'm going to turn around, keeping the barrel of my gun lowered to the ground, but I'm not going to drop it until I see that you are armed. I don't plan to give you my gun if you don't have one."

"Suit yourself."

Robert made the slow turn and was sorry to see that Wayne had a Glock pistol aimed at his chest. He had not been bluffing.

"Your gun. Drop it on the ground. Now."

Robert did as he was instructed.

"Good," Wayne said. "You have been spying on me since Sunday. While I was driving here from Chicago, I felt like I was being followed, but I wasn't sure. Did you follow me to this town?"

"Yes. I'm a private investigator from Chicago. I need to retrieve that briefcase that you are holding. My client is willing to pay you a large sum of money for its return."

"For an empty briefcase?" Wayne snapped open the briefcase and flipped it open. There was nothing inside.

"So you already have sold its contents?"

"Yes. It took a while, but the Internet is a very helpful tool in placing buyers and sellers together. I finalized the sale this morning."

"Then I will tell my client that it is too late."

"Your client is a powerful man who will come after me. And you will give him the information that he needs to get me."

"My client might have to flee this country since that briefcase has been compromised. His only interest now will be in saving himself. You don't need to worry about him."

Wayne said nothing and just stared at Robert for about ten seconds.

"May I leave?" Robert asked.

"Do you know what? You aren't the first private detective that I have met. I knew a guy in Los Angeles who was in your line of work. He was younger than you, but he was a lot like you. Do you understand what I mean? He was nosey, a busybody, always sticking his nose into other people's business."

"I am just trying to earn a living, man."

"Oh, is that what you were doing. I thought that you were sticking your nose into my business. Do you know how I earn my living?"

"I don't know."

"Sure you do. You know just about everything about me, and you're going to tell everything about me to your client."

"He was only interested in getting the briefcase back. That is the truth. Mr. Kirchner, it is getting very late, and I am tired. I would like to return to my hotel. May I leave?"

"Aren't you curious about how I knew that you were following me?"

"I suppose that I must have gotten careless."

"No, you did fine. You just didn't realize that I often follow my girlfriend around this town. After I got back from Chicago, she came to my apartment, and we had a good time doing what we like to do. When Sarah left my apartment, I followed her. She has no idea that I follow her. I figure that since she is cheating on her husband with me, she might start cheating on me with someone else. So far, though, I'm don't think that she has cheated on me, except with that gay guy that she married."

"I see."

"Yeah, well, anyway, as usual I followed her that evening. I was sure in for a surprise, though! As she walked down Main Street, I saw you begin tailing her. After you followed her for a few blocks, I thought that you were a rapist who was waiting for a good opportunity to attack her. However, when you didn't do anything to her, I realized that you were up to something else. I followed you back to your hotel."

"You did a good job. It never occurred to me that someone might follow me."

"I also followed you when you went to Angelique Plastiques. You must have gone there to talk to Tom Angelique. Did you tell him about me and his wife?"

"No."

"You are lying! You damned, lying snoop! Angelique had no idea that his wife was fooling around until you told him!"

"He didn't believe me." Robert realized that he was in great danger and that he needed to calm this unstable man.

"You might have ruined everything," Wayne almost hissed the words. "I have been planning for many months about how I'm going to get my hands on the Angelique fortune, and everything was going fine until a slimy snoop from Chicago stuck his nose where it didn't belong!"

"Take it easy, man. I didn't mess up any of your plans."

"Walk back through the woods toward the train tracks," Wayne ordered.

"So I can leave." Robert was momentarily hopeful that this confrontation would end well.

"Yes, but I'm going with you. Don't try anything or I'll shoot you."

Wayne walked several steps behind Robert, keeping the gun trained at Robert's head. They emerged from the woods and went toward the railroad tracks.

Wayne surveyed their surroundings. We are close to the edge of downtown; there are too many persons nearby to shoot him here. Someone would hear the gunshot. I need to purchase a silencer for my pistol, Wayne resolved. The next time that I'm in Chicago that's going to be my top priority.

Unseen by Robert, Wayne pulled a knife out of the sheath attached to his belt. Wayne now held the gun in his left hand, and the knife in his right hand. I can kill him silently with the knife, Wayne thought as he finalized his plan. The body will fall forward onto the railroad tracks. A train will come along within an hour or two and run him over. It will look like he committed suicide by laying down on the tracks.

"Stop here!" Wayne commanded as soon as they reached the edge of the tracks.

"Why?" Robert was very nervous, but he did not see any way that he could escape.

"Just stop." Wayne's voice seemed less stressed. Wayne took a step forward, his hand tightening on the handle of the knife as he prepared to make the fatal strike.

"Hey!" a man's voice shouted from about forty yards away. "Hey, you guys!"

Startled, Wayne slipped the knife back into his belt sheath. He pressed the pistol into Robert's back and out of view of the approaching man.

"Keep quiet if you want to live," Wayne whispered to Robert.

Wayne turned to see a tall man in a park ranger uniform emerging from the woods and walking toward them.

"This area is closed after sunset," the man called to them. He came to a stop about ten yards from Wayne and Robert.

"I'm sorry. We didn't know." Wayne wondered whether the man had seen either of his weapons.

"That's okay. It's a new regulation. There has been a problem with teenagers hanging around and drinking out here at night."

"We are heading back downtown anyway. Thanks for letting us know about the regulation."

"No problem." The man walked back toward the woods. "Have a good evening, gentleman."

"Thanks!" Wayne waved good-bye and then told Robert, "Walk across the tracks and head toward Main Street."

As the two men crossed the railroad tracks, Wayne placed the pistol back into the shoulder holster beneath his jacket. They went through the small park and onto the downtown streets.

"You should buy a lottery ticket tonight, man," Wayne told Robert. "This is your lucky night!"

"May I leave?"

"Yes, but don't ever follow me again. And tell your client in Chicago to leave me alone. He will be sorry if he comes after me."

"I will give him that message," Robert said.

"Okay. So long, dude," Wayne said and watched Robert walk away along the downtown street toward his hotel.

Wayne shook his head in disbelief that Robert was still alive. I was within three seconds of killing him. That is one lucky guy. What were the odds of a park ranger coming along at that moment?

As he headed toward Main Street, Wayne glanced back toward the woods, but the person who had saved Robert was nowhere to be seen.

CHAPTER 12

I could use a drink, Wayne thought as he looked over at the bar on the corner. He walked toward the bar, then paused when he spotted a familiar face coming down Main Street about a block away. What is Sarah doing downtown this evening? Is she coming to see me? No, she's going in the opposite direction from my place.

The bar was immediately forgotten. Wayne followed Sarah for about two blocks. He watched as she went up the steps of St. Faustina Church and went inside.

Wayne snarled at a couple of persons who said "Good evening" to him as he stomped through the downtown streets.

He walked up the front steps of St. Faustina Church. He paused before going inside, feeling both an attraction and revulsion toward the church. For several seconds, the feelings of revulsion were so strong that he started to go back down the steps toward the street.

Then he remembered why he had come, pushed back his distaste about entering the church, and went back up the steps. He resisted the inclination to turn around again and pushed open the door.

Wayne did not want Sarah to see him, so he remained in the vestibule. He looked through one of the vestibule windows and could see Sarah standing near the wall. Why doesn't she sit down in one of the pews? He was briefly puzzled, then noticed the door near where she was standing. Wayne then understood: she was waiting to go to confession.

Wayne was briefly amused by the idea of Sarah telling all of her carnal sins to the priest. Then it occurred to him that this priest was likely an important reason for the recent changes in Sarah. Wayne felt rage growing within him. The priest might cause me to lose Sarah.

A woman emerged from the confessional, and Sarah went inside. Believing that he had discovered what he wanted to know, Wayne decided that he might as well leave.

He stormed out of the church and headed toward the corner bar where he sat and drank in sullen silence for about twenty minutes. I'm not going to allow that priest to ruin everything for me, Wayne resolved, slamming down his glass. He is another damned busybody! He's just like that private investigator. I will show that priest what happens to people who don't mind their own business!

Wayne left the bar and went back to the church. Sarah will be gone by now, he thought as he walked up the front steps.

Wayne entered the church and looked around cynically. There were about five persons in the pews and a man standing against the wall near a wooden door of the confessional.

He sat down in the back pew and watched. After a couple of minutes, a women emerged from the confessional and the man who was waiting went inside. The man's confession last about four minutes. When he came out, the man went into a pew and knelt down.

I guess it's my turn, Wayne thought as he got up, walked into the confessional, and closed the door. He was momentarily confused; it appeared that the room was empty. However, then Wayne realized that the priest was seated behind the two-foot-wide screen.

Wayne went over to the other side and stood next to the empty chair for penitents.

"Good evening," Father Kinsella said. When Wayne continued to stand there without saying anything, the priest gestured toward the chair. "Have a seat."

Wayne hesitated, then sat down.

"God is glad that you are here. You can proceed with your confession, son."

"So this is when I'm supposed to tell you about what a bad boy I've been?"

"Yes, you can tell your sins now."

"I am not a Catholic, Father."

"Well, that's fine. I occasionally have non-Catholics come here. I will be happy to talk to you, but you can't actually receive the sacrament of penance until you become a Catholic. Although I'm not able to grant sacramental absolution to non-Catholics, it is fine if you want to tell me your sins. I will offer some advice and then give you a blessing."

"That sure is nice of you. You and I have a mutual friend, Father. Sarah Angelique. I hear that she came here to talk to you earlier this evening. I'm Wayne, her boyfriend."

Father Kinsella's expression did not change. "Hello, Wayne."

"I'm sure that Sarah told you all about me."

"Wayne, I would like to help you. If you want to talk about some of your problems or struggles in life, perhaps I could give you some advice or guidance that might be helpful."

"I'm not going to tell you my sins. I don't believe in sin. I believe in living life to its fullest. Talking to you in this little room is ridiculous."

"Then why are here this evening?"

Wayne stood up. "I came here to tell you to mind your own business! Sarah is mine; she belongs to me, not to that wimp that she married!"

"I will pray for you, Wayne. Good evening." Father Kinsella looked down at the book that he had been reading while waiting for penitents to arrive.

"You can't get rid of me that easily, Padre," Wayne said loudly.

Wayne stepped forward, grabbed the priest's black shirt just below the Roman collar, and shoved him against the wall.

"You are going to keep your mouth shut about what Sarah told you, priest! Do you understand?"

With strength that surprised Wayne, Father Kinsella grabbed his two arms and pushed him backwards, causing Wayne to bump into the penitent's chair. Father Kinsella walked around the screen toward the door.

"Once again, I bid you good evening, Wayne," the priest said firmly.

"Damn you!" Wayne shouted. "I'm going to burn down this church with you inside of it!"

"Father Kinsella, are you all right in there?" one of the parishioners called from outside the door. Several of them had heard the commotion.

As the priest started to go out the door, Wayne lurched at him and threw a right hook punch that struck Father Kinsella's jaw. He fell back against the door, which swung open. Momentarily stunned by the blow, the priest toppled onto the floor.

Three concerned parishioners stared in wide-eyed surprise at him, then in horror at the Wayne who strode forward menacingly.

Wayne glared at them. "What are you looking at, old man? Get out of here, grandpa!"

Standing near the elderly man, a middle-aged woman pulled out her cell phone to call the police.

"Drop that phone!" Wayne commanded.

When she did not obey immediately, Wayne pulled out the Glock pistol and aimed it at her. "I said to drop that damn phone!"

Terrified, she tossed the phone onto the floor.

"Don't shoot us!" a young, red-haired woman screamed, her eyes wide with fear.

"I will shoot you if you don't shut up!" Wayne shouted at her.

Father Kinsella had stood up. "There is no need to shoot anyone, Wayne."

Wayne aimed the gun at the priest's chest. "You meddling, busybody! You remind me of another snoop that I know. That snoop almost got killed this evening. Mind your own business, priest, or you will end up dead."

Wayne glanced across the church. There were two other persons in pews watching what was happening. This is attracting way too much attention, he realized. I should never have come here this evening. I lost control of my temper again. I used to be able to control it better.

Wayne put the pistol back into the holster beneath his jacket. I'd better get out of here, he told himself. As he walked rapidly out of the church, he glared back at the priest and his parishioners in order to make sure that no one followed him.

About seven minutes later, Sergeant John Cantillon and two other police officers arrived. They took statements from everyone who had witnessed the incident.

"Are you sure that you don't want to go to the hospital, Father?" Sergeant Cantillon asked.

"Yes, I'm sure. I'm fine. I will have a couple of bruises in the morning, but I am not injured."

"Do you know the man who struck you?"

"No. This was the first time that I saw him."

"Why was he so angry with you?"

"Apparently he did not appreciate some advice that I gave."

"Which was?"

"I am actually limited in what I can say here. The seal of confession prevents me from revealing information that I obtained while administering the sacrament of reconciliation. However, the man who caused the trouble here tonight was not Catholic and did not attempt to make a sincere confession, so I can talk about him. He said that his first name is Wayne. He has a good right hook and a bad temper."

"What advice did you give that ticked him off so much?"

"His anger toward me relates to the confession of another person, so I cannot say anything about that confession."

"I understand," Sergeant Cantillon said. "I thought that confessions were only held on Saturday afternoon. I didn't know that you also had them in the evenings."

"Just this one evening every week. Some persons work on Saturday afternoon or for other reasons find that time inconvenient. Father Dorsey and I wanted to make the sacrament of penance more easily available for everyone, so we decided to add on these evening confessions. It has been successful, and we've been pleased with the results."

"Until this evening."

"Well, things like this will happen from time to time, but I can assure you that we will be continuing with evening confessions."

"That's good, Father." Sergeant Cantillon closed his notebook. "Well, we should be able to track down this thug. I'd better get back out on the streets and start searching for him."

The priest thanked the sergeant and two other officers who were soon out on the downtown streets in search of Wayne.

Chapter 13

The front lawn of the church looked like a scene from a postcard as snow fell on the manger of the Nativity scene that had just been placed on the lawn the previous day. Two spotlights illuminated the all-white figures of the Holy Family and the three wise men who neared the completion of a long journey.

Father Kinsella walked across the lawn as he headed toward the rectory. He saw Sarah hurrying down the street in his direction.

"Hello, Sarah," he said as she came up the hill and approached him.

"Father, are you all right? I'm so sorry! I just heard what happened!"

"I'm fine. There is no need to worry."

"Thank you for not mentioning my name to the police."

"Oh, I would never reveal any information that was given to me during the sacrament of penance. As you know, the seal of confession is absolute."

"Can I make a confession now?"

"Sure. We can either go back into the church or you could just make your confession now while we walk."

"This will be fine." She paused to collect her thoughts, then resumed, "Bless me, Father, for I have sinned. It has been several weeks since my last confession. During this period I committed adultery a couple of times. However, I am going to end the affair with Wayne. I will never commit adultery again."

"I'm glad to hear that you have made the decision to end the adulterous affair, Sarah."

"Yes. I now see with complete clarity what a creep Wayne is; I was a fool not to see it sooner. And he has gotten worse in the last couple of months. He has become a heavy drug user, and he is also selling drugs. He has also started to carry a pistol and a knife."

"Wayne is a very dangerous man, Sarah. You will need to be very careful."

"About a half hour ago, I called the police anonymously from a pay phone. I don't want to bring scandal to my parents or to Tom or to the Angelique family, so I have to do this anonymously."

"That seems like a prudent decision."

"Thanks. I gave the police Wayne's name and address, and I told them that he has drugs and an unregistered handgun there along with thousands of dollars in cash from his crimes. I didn't like turning him in to the police, but I know that he is going to try to hurt me unless he is behind bars. The drugs are warping his brain."

Father Kinsella nodded. "Until Wayne is in custody, you will need to be on your guard. If he is not arrested right away, he might guess that you reported him and come after you."

"I will be careful, Father," she promised.

"Perhaps you and Tom could take a road trip for a few days until he is arrested."

"That sounds like a good idea."

Sarah said an Act of Contrition prayer, and the priest granted her absolution.

They had completely circled the church grounds as they walked back onto the front lawn.

"Thanks for everything, Father," Sarah said as she waved good-bye.

"You're very welcome. Good luck, Sarah."

While Sarah was speaking with Father Kinsella, Wayne was a few miles away. He was sitting in his car as he waited on the parking lot of the corporate headquarters of Angelique Plastiques.

Sarah has changed, Wayne reflected. She used to be wild and a free spirit. Now she is Miss Prim-and-Proper. It's the fault of that priest. Just like that private investigator, the priest doesn't know how to mind his own business. I should put a bullet in the priest's head.

No, killing a priest would attract too much attention. And another priest would just take his place. One busybody would be replaced by another busybody. There is no end to them.

Sarah's husband is probably also responsible for the change in her. Wayne glanced across the parking lot at the entrance to Angelique Plastiques. When is this guy going to leave work?

I can't believe that I have to do this by myself. It would be so easy for Sarah to kill him. He never goes to bars, so I have no way to slip something into his drink. Sarah could do it so easily at their home.

Wayne had considered cutting the brake line in Tom's car. However, most of the area near the headquarters was flat land with little traffic. If the brakes on his car failed after he left work, it was unlikely that the crash would be fatal. In fact, he might not crash at all. When he realized that he had no brakes, Tom could simply turn onto an open field and coast to a stop.

Wayne knew that it was possible to attach a small remote-controlled device to the brake line and then activate it when the target was driving near a cliff or when approaching a red light at a busy intersection. Wayne did not have such a device, though, and he did not know where to purchase one. He also realized that he lacked the technical knowledge to install such a device.

No, I am going to keep things simple today. I have followed him home four times, and he always takes the same route. Just what I would expect from a boring guy like him. On his route home, there is only one good place to cause a fatal accident.

Wayne was slouched in the driver's seat, but he sat upright when he spotted Tom coming out of the building. Tom walked to his car, backed out of the parking spot, and headed down the driveway.

It's showtime, Wayne thought as he followed Tom onto the road. Wayne kept back about a quarter mile so that Tom would not notice him. I know exactly where he is going anyway, so it doesn't matter if I lose sight of him, Wayne reflected.

When Tom turned onto a road that went up a fairly high hill, Wayne made his move. He accelerated and got much closer to Tom's car. At this point it doesn't matter whether he notices me or not. He will soon be a dead man.

Wayne was happy that there were no other cars on the road—no one to get in the way and no witnesses. As he moved directly behind Tom's car, Wayne saw Tom glance into his rearview mirror. Too late, Tommy Boy.

Wayne accelerated and slammed into the back of Tom's car. He will probably want to stop and exchange insurance cards, Wayne smirked as he pressed the accelerator almost to the floor.

Tom pressed hard on his own accelerator and grasped the steering wheel tightly as he attempted to keep control of his car. He immediately realized that this was no accident. That maniac intentionally crashed into me, Tom realized.

As Tom neared the summit of the hill, Wayne swung around to the left, pulled alongside Tom's car, and sideswiped him. Wayne wanted to knock Tom over the cliff at the top of the hill. It was unlikely anyone could survive such a fall.

Just as Wayne was about to sideswiped him still harder, Tom slammed on his brakes and made a quick U-turn. Tom sped back down the hill.

After making a similar U-turn, Wayne resumed his pursuit. He was furious that he had missed making the kill at his chosen spot and cursed Tom for wrecking his plan.

Once again Wayne slammed into the back of Tom's car, but Tom managed to keep control. Both men narrowly avoided hitting a SUV that had to swerve out of their way.

At the bottom of the hill, Tom turned back onto the roadway leading toward his company. He grabbed his cell phone and started to call the police.

Wayne saw that Tom was making a call, and he saw persons in other cars and pedestrians looking at them. He realized that this was attracting way too much attention.

I need to end this now, Wayne thought. He accelerated alongside Tom's car and then swerved hard to the right. As the sides of the two cards smashed together, it became impossible for Tom to keep control of his car, which went sliding into a ditch and turned over.

Wayne almost went into the ditch also, but he swung hard to the left at the last instant and managed to keep his damaged car on the road.

I have to get out of here, Wayne told himself. The police are probably already on their way. He went speeding away, uncertain whether his mission had been successful.

Tom's car was upside down in the ditch. The car's front and side airbags had deployed, preventing Tom from being seriously injured or killed. His seatbelt kept him secured in place, but he was now upside down in the car. He was dazed by the impact and lost consciousness for a few seconds.

After about a minute, Tom unfastened his seatbelt and opened the car door. Just as he was climbing out of the car, a police car and ambulance were pulling up alongside of him. Seeing blood on his shirt and his groggy condition, the attendants placed him in the ambulance and were soon heading toward the hospital.

CHAPTER 14

Thirty minutes later Sarah was rushing down the hospital hallway. Breathlessly, she hurried over to an information counter.

"Someone from the hospital called me a few minutes ago. She said that my husband, Thomas Angelique, had been brought here. He was in a car accident."

The woman at the counter typed his name into her computer. "Oh, yes. Your husband is listed in good condition, Mrs. Angelique. He was just taken from the Emergency Room to Room 313."

"Thank you." Sarah was relieved to hear this news. For the past half-hour, she had been afraid that he was going to die. The intensity of her fear about losing Tom made her realize how very much she wanted to keep him.

After taking the elevator to the third floor, Sarah quickly found his room. She entered to find Tom alone in the room, his eyes closed as he rested in bed. Thinking that he was asleep, Sarah did not say anything. She sat down in the chair next to his bed, placing her purse on the floor. Tears filling her eyes as she looked at him.

Tom opened his eyes and turned to look at her. "Hey, Beautiful."

Sarah leaned forward and placed her hand on his arm. "Oh, Tom! How are you feeling?"

"Pretty good. I have a headache and a few bruises, but I seem to be fine. They initially thought that I might have a concussion, but now they don't think so."

"What happened?"

"Some crazy guy tried to kill me with his car. I was on my way home from work when he began ramming me with his car. Apparently, it was a case of road rage. However, I have no idea what I did to tick this guy off. I never even noticed his car until I was going up the hill on Belleville Road toward our subdivision."

Sarah had a sinking feeling in her stomach. She strongly suspected that she knew the identity of the attacker.

"What did the driver look like?"

"It all happened so fast that I didn't get a good look at him. He was young, probably in his twenties. And I think that he had a mustache. I wasn't able to get the license number of his car. Hopefully, one of the witnesses was able to get his license number."

"Let's hope so." Sarah said. She did not need the license number, though.

Wayne will pay for trying to kill Tom and for attacking Father Kinsella, Sarah thought with pure fury. I'm going to make sure that he receives the justice that he deserves.

"Is everything okay?" Tom asked. He had noticed the fire in her eyes.

"Yes. Everything is wonderful now that I know that you aren't badly hurt. I'm going to run down to the snack bar. Do you want me to bring anything up to you?"

"Yeah. I'd like either a Dr. Pepper or a Pepsi."

"Okay, dear. I will be back soon."

Sarah walked down the hallway and took the elevator down to the lobby. She sat down on a couch and used her cell phone to call Wayne.

After three rings, he answered, "Hi, baby."

"Hello, Wayne, you have been busy today." She tried to keep the fury out of her voice.

"Yeah. I'm sorry about going after him without telling you, but you just couldn't bring yourself to do what needed to be done. I figured that you would be pleased after it was all over."

"I am. But I'm still in shock."

"Is he dead?"

"Yes, but we shouldn't be talking about this on the phone. I will meet you at your apartment. Are you there now?"

"No. The cops raided it early today. I was driving home when I saw two patrol cars parked by my building. I got out of the area in a hurry, and I called one of my neighbors. She said that the police had a search warrant and found drugs in my apartment."

"How did they know about what you were doing?" Sarah asked. Perhaps my phone call to them telling them about the drugs had something to do with it, she added silently.

"I'm not sure. There was a private investigator snooping around my apartment building the other day. It might have had something to do with him."

"I see."

"Fortunately, most of my China white supply was hidden safely in my car, and I have my Glock pistol with me."

"Since we can't go to your apartment, let's meet somewhere else. How about the McDonald's on Main Street?"

"No. I don't want to go anywhere near downtown. There are too many people and too many police around. And my car is badly damaged. I'm going to have to ditch that car somewhere and get a rental car."

"Where do you want to meet?"

"Let's meet on the parking lot of Angelique Plastiques in about an hour. There won't be many persons there in the evening."

"Okay. I'll see you there in an hour."

"Everything's going to be great now, baby."

"Right. See you later, Wayne."

Sarah hung up her cell phone and walked across the lobby to the pay phone to call the police. She did not want to use her cell phone because she wanted to remain anonymous.

"Hello, this is 911," the operator answered.

"Hi, I called earlier today to report a drug dealer named Wayne Kirchner. The police should have used unmarked cars when they went to raid his apartment. He saw them and got away. A short while ago, I found out that he tried to kill one of your town's most prominent citizens today. Wayne Kirchner is the person who crashed his car into Thomas Angelique's car. If the police had caught him when they were supposed to, Mr. Angelique would not have been injured."

"May I ask your name, Miss?"

"I prefer to remain anonymous. Wayne Kirchner is a very dangerous man. I have just learned that he is planning on getting a rental car this evening because his own car is so badly damaged. Wayne Kirchner will be on the parking lot of Angelique Plastiques in about an hour."

"May I ask how you obtained this information?"

"He told me that he would be there. And this time the police need to be more careful. They should have officers in plainclothes and unmarked cars trap him on the Angelique parking lot. I should also tell you that he has a gun and is very violent. Your officers need to be very careful. They will probably need to shoot him."

After providing the 911 operator with a detailed description of Wayne's damaged car, Sarah said good-bye and hung up.

I hope that the police kill Wayne, she reflected. I really do. There is a battle between good and evil in this world, and Wayne is definitely on the side of evil. He would never repent and reform; in fact, he is getting more evil every day. Hopefully the police will be more careful this time and not allow him to get away again.

Sarah went over to the snack bar and purchased two cans of soda, which she took back up to the third floor to Tom's room.

CHAPTER 15

When she entered the room, she was surprised to see a golden-haired child sitting in the chair next to Tom's bed, speaking to him.

"Well, hello there," Sarah said to the girl.

"Sarah, this is my new friend, Chloe," Tom said.

"Hello Chloe."

"Hi Sarah." The girl held out her right hand and shook hands with Sarah.

"Aren't you the cutest little thing?" Sarah smiled broadly. She then spotted the wagon next to the chair.

At that moment, Sarah realized that this was the girl that she had seen in the hospital hallway about three months earlier when Sarah brought her mother to the hospital for a weekly treatment.

"Chloe gave me two very nice presents." Tom held up a sleeve of golf balls. "I can put these to good use, and the golf balls are even embossed with the hospital logo!" Then Tom lifted up a foot-high framed photo of a several golfers standing on the ocean-side putting green on a beautiful golf course. "I think that this is the Pebble

Beach course. I'm going to hang this photo near my desk in the study!"

"Those are wonderful gifts for Tom, Chloe. He often plays golf at the country club."

Chloe reached into the wagon and pulled out a pink parasol. "This is for you, Sarah."

"You are so sweet! But you don't need to give me a present."

"I want you to have it." Chloe handed her the parasol.

"Thank you very much. It's beautiful."

"I have a picture for you, too." Chloe gave her a foot-high framed photo of a woman snorkeling near some coral reefs with many tropical fish around her.

"This is great!" Sarah declared. "In August I went snorkeling in the Pacific Ocean, and in September I went scuba diving in the Atlantic Ocean. This will be a wonderful reminder of my undersea adventures!"

"Good," Chloe said. "I hope that the picture also makes you think about another sea that is far deeper and vaster than both the Pacific and Atlantic oceans. And you don't need to travel a long way to reach it. This sea is always nearby and you just need to choose to enter it."

"I don't know what sea to which you are referring," Sarah said. "Is this a riddle, Chloe?"

"Kind of."

"Well, I give up. What is this vast sea?"

Chloe chuckled. "You can think about it for a while. I'll tell you in a day or two."

"You are as cute as can be." Sarah smiled at her.

"Where did you get these pretty framed pictures, Chloe?" Tom asked.

"When my Gram and I were downtown a couple of weeks ago, we bought them at a photography shop on Main Street."

"Well, they are great presents," Tom said. "And I can't wait to try out my new golf balls when the weather gets warmer. Thank you very much!"

"I will also always treasure both of my presents, Chloe," Sarah said.

Chloe looked very pleased that her gifts had been so well received.

"Just before you came back to the room, Chloe was telling me that she delivers presents to all the children in this hospital," Tom said. "She has been doing this great work for many months."

"I also give presents to some adults, but I don't always have enough stuff for everyone. I have given away all my toys, but my grandmother lets me buy more stuff when I go shopping with her. Sometimes I buy presents in the gift shop downstairs, but their prices are kind of high."

Sarah smiled. "Yes, gift shops often have very cute things, but they do tend to be expensive."

"Chloe is Santa's little helper," Tom said.

"She certainly is. She is the most unselfish child that I have ever met. Did you say that you even gave away your own toys?"

"Yes. I'm very sick, and I will be going to Heaven soon. I live with my Gram, but she doesn't play with toys."

Sarah was startled by this news. She hesitated for a moment before replying. "I'm sorry to hear that you are ill, Chloe. However, this hospital has some very good doctors. They might be able to help you get better."

"Oh, I'm not afraid of dying. When I was four years old, my parents were killed in a car accident. That's why my Gram is raising me. I'm looking forward to being with my parents in Heaven forever. That's our true home."

"Sarah and I will both pray for you, Chloe," Tom said.

"Thank you. Look what I have." Chloe pulled from her pocket a multi-colored rosary. "This is called a mission rosary. Father Kinsella gave it to me and taught me how to say the rosary. Each group of ten beads is a different color—red, blue, green, white, and gold. Archbishop Fulton Sheen was the person who created the mission rosary. Each color represents a different region of the world, so you pray for the success of Catholic missions everywhere when you say the rosary."

"That's wonderful, Chloe," Tom said. "Sarah and I are members of St. Faustina parish, so we know both Father Kinsella and Father Dorsey."

"Chloe, about three months ago, I brought my mother to this hospital for her cancer treatments. When I was in the waiting room, I saw you walking down the hallway with your wagon. I almost went down the hall to talk to you. You looked so familiar to me. I didn't know where I had seen you previously. Since you go to St. Faustina Church, I am thinking that might be why you look so familiar. I've probably seen you at Mass."

"Maybe. My Gram and I do go to Mass there sometimes. We more often go to St. Thomas Aquinas Church and to St. Jude Thaddeus Church, though." Chloe got a wide smile on her face. "I bet that you remember me from somewhere else."

"Where?" Sarah asked.

"When you were crowned as the Snow Maiden, my Gram and I were standing in the front row. We watched you win."

"That's it!" Sarah exclaimed. "And you had your wagon with you! I remember you!"

"I wanted you to win," Chloe said. "It was very important that you become the Snow Maiden."

"Why?"

"So that everything would work out the way that it is supposed to work out."

"How do you know these things, Chloe?"

"That's what my Gram always asks me. I just somehow know things."

A nurse stuck her head in the door.

"Chloe, there you are! I wondered who you were visiting. It is time for your medicine, young lady. You need to go back to your room."

"Yes, Molly." Chloe scrambled down from the chair and grabbed the handle of her almost-empty wagon. "See you later, alligators," she waved to Tom and Sarah.

"I'll pop in your room later to say goodnight to you, sweetheart," Sarah told Chloe as she went out the door.

"Chloe is our social butterfly," the nurse said. "She visits everyone, and everyone loves her—especially the other children. And I don't know how she keeps coming up with all those presents for everyone—her wagon seems to magically replenish itself."

"Chloe indicated that she is very ill," Tom said. "Is that correct?"

The nurse nodded. "Yes. She has been fighting cancer for a long time. We don't understand how she stays so active and in such good spirits."

"Is there any type of experimental treatment that could be tried?" Tom asked. "I have only known Chloe for less than a half-hour, but I'm so impressed with her that I would be willing to pay for any treatment might help her. Even if the treatment is very expensive and only offers a remote chance, I will pay for it."

"That is very generous of you, Mr. Angelique, but everything has already been tried. Chloe has been in and out of this hospital for over a year. Several doctors donated pro bono services. These treatments probably extended her life."

Tom and Sarah spoke with the nurse for a couple of more minutes. The nurse told Tom that the doctor wanted him to stay overnight for observation, but Tom could go home in the morning.

After the nurse left, Sarah went back down to the lobby. She called the police from the pay phone.

"Hello, I called earlier to report that a drug dealer named Wayne Kirchner was going to be on the parking lot of Angelique Plastiques this evening. He is the man who tried to kill Mr. Thomas Angelique earlier today. I wanted to know whether Wayne Kirchner was captured?"

"One moment please," the 911 operator said. "Sergeant Cantillon would like to speak with you."

After a few seconds, the police sergeant said, "Hello, this is John Cantillon. I understand that you are the lady who has been helping us out today."

"Yes, and I am hoping that Wayne Kirchner has been arrested."

"Unfortunately, he didn't show up on the Angelique Plastiques parking lot. We did find his car on a side street a few miles from there. Apparently he abandoned the car. The trunk and glove compartment were almost empty. We also found some secret compartments beneath the seats that we assume that he used to conceal drug shipments. The compartments were empty, but we found traces of heroin."

"Darn it!" Sarah felt extremely frustrated. "Did you check with the local car rental places?"

"Yes. Wayne Kirchner did rent a car, and we know the make, model and license number. I'm optimistic that we will have him in custody soon."

Sarah relaxed a bit. "That's good."

"It would be helpful if you would come in and tell us everything that you know."

"No. I want to remain anonymous. The only other useful thing that I could tell you is his cell phone number. Perhaps you could call him and pretend that you want to buy some heroin." Sarah gave the police sergeant Wayne's cell phone number.

"Thank you, but I still wish that you would come into the station. Or at least give me your name."

"I'm sorry, Sergeant. This way is for the best."

"All right."

"Perhaps you could use cell phone triangulation to track down Wayne Kirchner," Sarah suggested. "I have seen it done on television programs."

"That might be possible. I'll see what we can do."

"Great. Good luck, good-bye."

Sarah hung up, disappointed that Wayne was not in custody, but encouraged that the police seemed to be closing in on him.

She glanced across the lobby at the gift shop and was glad to see that it had not yet closed for the evening. Sarah went into the shop and grabbed a basket off the counter; she knew that she was going to make many purchases.

She bought books for both children and adults, jewelry, toys, games, playing cards, candy, and various knickknacks.

Chapter 16

Sarah carried the shopping bags filled with her purchases over to an elevator, went up to a nursing station, and asked for Chloe's room number. As it turned out, Chloe was just down the hall from Tom.

Peeking into the room, Sarah was glad to see that Chloe was still awake.

"Knock, knock."

"Hi, Sarah! Come on in." Chloe sat up, swinging her legs over the side of the bed.

Sarah sat in the chair facing her and presented the shopping bags.

"Everything in these bags is for you, Chloe. I noticed that your wagon was getting a bit low, so I decided to re-supply you."

"Thank you so much, Sarah!" Chloe declared with great enthusiasm as she eagerly searched through the bags of treasure.

"You don't have to give away everything, dear. You can keep anything that you want from those bags."

"Oh, I will give it all away, but I'm going to read these two pop-up books first before I give them away." Chloe looked at the covers of the **Alice in Wonderland** and the **Wizard of Oz** pop-up books.

Sarah noticed Chloe wince slightly as she adjusted her sitting position on the bed.

"Are you in much pain, Chloe?"

"Not right now, but sometimes it is bad." Chloe picked up the multi-colored rosary that she had shown Sarah and Tom earlier that evening. "That is one of the reasons that Father Kinsella gave me this rosary and taught me about it. These are the sorrowful mysteries. When I am sad or afraid, I think about how Jesus felt in the Garden of Gethsemane. When the pain gets bad, I think about how Jesus was beaten, crowned with thorns, had to carry the Cross, and had to die. There is a bead for each event, for each mystery.

"Father said that I can unite myself to Jesus through the rosary's sorrowful mysteries." Her hands moved across the beads with a practiced familiarity. "And these beads, the Glorious mysteries, remind me that I will rise from the dead and be in Heaven with Jesus. And I will be with my father and mother just as Jesus ascended into Heaven to be with His Father and the Holy Spirit and with Mary and Joseph."

"That's wonderful, dear," Sarah said. "I have never said a rosary, but I will say one soon. The stained glass windows at St. Faustina Church depict all of the rosary mysteries, so I can look at those windows to remind me about all twenty mysteries."

"My Gram took me over to St. Faustina Church this afternoon. I wanted to see the manger scene and the other Christmas decorations. Tomorrow evening Gram is going to drive me around town to look at Christmas lights."

"Oh, I love to look at Christmas lights. Tom and I need to get up our display. He bought some of those giant inflatable decorations."

"Those giant inflatables are great!" Chloe declared enthusiastically. "Last December I saw a house that had a Winnie-the-Pooh inflatable. And there was another house that had an inflatable snowglobe with Rudolph the Red-Nosed Reindeer with his friends Hermey the elf, Yukon the prospector, and the abominable snowman. And the blowing snow makes it look like they're in a blizzard!"

"That sounds adorable," Sarah said. "I'm not sure what inflatable Tom purchased. However, after talking to you, I can hardly wait to see them!"

"I bet that they will be beautiful!" Chloe giggled.

"I'm not sure how soon we will get up our decorations, but I'll give you our address so that you and your grandmother can stop by to see our Christmas display. And be sure to ring our doorbell and come inside for some cookies and cocoa!"

"Okay!"

Sarah took a piece of paper out of her purse and wrote her address and phone number on it. She handed it to Chloe.

"Thanks, Sarah." Chloe placed the paper into her own purse, which was on the nightstand by the bed.

After speaking together for a few more minutes, Sarah kissed Chloe goodnight and returned to Tom's room.

CHAPTER 17

The next morning Sarah drove Tom home from the hospital. She fried some bacon and eggs for both Tom and herself. After they had eaten, they went into the living room to relax and read the newspaper.

"How are you feeling, Tom?" Sarah asked after they had been in the living room for about a half hour.

"Great. Maybe I'll go into work this afternoon."

"Don't even think about it, Mister."

"I'm just kidding. Actually, I will probably also stay home tomorrow, too. I'm sort of between projects right now, so this is a good time for me to take off. My sister approved my charitable projects idea. In many different cities, we are going to begin working with faith-based charities to provide training and jobs for homeless persons. And we are also going to dramatically increase the annual donations that we are making to Catholic missionaries."

"That's wonderful, Tom." Sarah paused, deep in thought. "I have something that I need to tell you, but it can wait. Perhaps I should wait until you get back to full strength."

"Wow, talk about piquing my curiosity!" Tom laughed. "I feel fine, Sarah. Come on—out with it. What's on your mind?"

"You aren't going to like this one bit. In fact, I wasn't planning on ever telling you because I didn't want to hurt you. However, after what happened yesterday, I feel that I need to tell you."

Seeing her concern, Tom became more serious. "Sarah, you can tell me anything. I love you, and we can get through anything together. What is it?"

Tears filled Sarah's eyes. "I thought that I could tell you, but I can't." She turned away from him.

Tom went over to stand in front of her. "Does this have to do with Wayne Kirchner?"

Sarah looked up at him, her eyes wide. "Where did you hear that name?"

"A couple of days ago a man named Robert Alma showed up at my office. He said that he was a private detective from Chicago and that he had followed Wayne Kirchner here. Apparently, Kirchner had stolen from his client a briefcase containing important information. He had Kirchner's apartment under surveillance and was planning to break in to retrieve the briefcase. During his stakeout, he saw you visiting the apartment building. Mr. Alma showed me photos of you going into the building. He did some research and found out that you and Kirchner attended college together in California.

"Mr. Alma wanted me to hire him to follow you, but I declined his offer. He thought that you were having an affair with Kirchner. I hoped that you weren't."

Sarah was amazed that Tom had this much information. The fact that he already knew this much made it somewhat easier for her to continue.

"Wayne Kirchner and I dated during my last two years of college in California. After graduation, he followed me back here. We continued sleeping together even after you and I began dating and became engaged. I liked you very much, but he was a bad habit that I could not break."

Tom stared at her, struggling to keep his composure. "Why did you marry me, Sarah?"

"After my father lost his job and my mother became so ill, my family was in a desperate financial situation. I have to admit that the main reason that I wanted to marry you was because you were wealthy and could solve my parent's financial problems. And you did. You were the heroic knight who saved us all.

"However, I was selfish and immature, and I continued to have sex with Wayne even after we were married. I am so sorry that I committed adultery. I sinned against God and against you."

Sarah paused in order to give Tom a chance to speak. When he remained silent, she continued, "When we were college students, Wayne and I used to pull a scam in which we would place a pill called a "roofie" into the drink of a businessman that we met in nightclubs and casinos. After the man passed out, we would steal his money."

"How could you do such a thing?" Tom asked.

"I don't know. I made some awful decisions."

"Becoming involved with Wayne was certainly an awful decision," Tom said, raising his voice but not shouting. "Why would you become involved with someone so evil?"

"I always realized that Wayne was not a good man, but I only recently began to see clearly how evil he is. I think that he has become worse in the last few months. His use of drugs has probably contributed to this decline."

"I'm disappointed in you, Sarah."

She began to cry. "You are the last person in the world that I wanted to disappoint. I'm so sorry. I'm disappointed in myself."

Seeing her distress, Tom's anger dissipated. He reached over and wiped the tears off her face.

"Don't cry, Sarah. All will be well."

"I hope so." She was glad that Tom had a calm personality; she knew that some men would have become violently angry.

"So when did Wayne decide to try to kill me?"

"Wayne told me a few weeks ago that he wanted to cause you to have a fatal accident so that I would inherit everything as well as get your insurance money. He wanted me to share this money with him so that he could become a millionaire.

"Of course, I rejected this idea, and I haven't seen him much recently. I was about to completely end the affair. Then I heard that he went to St. Faustina Church and struck Father Kinsella. He somehow knew that I had been getting advice from Father. I suppose that he must have followed me when I went to confession last week.

"I was furious about the attack on Father Kinsella. At that moment the affair was completely over. In fact, I wanted Wayne to be sent to prison. I called the police anonymously and told them that Wayne was a heroin dealer. He had started selling it a couple of months ago. I told the police that Wayne had heroin and a gun in his apartment, and I gave them the address. The police raided the apartment and found the drugs, but Wayne was not there.

"When I heard the details of the attack on you yesterday, I realized that Wayne had decided to act on his own. He must have thought that if he caused you to have a fatal accident, I would go ahead and share the inheritance with him.

"He could not have been more wrong. I tried again to help the police catch him. I called Wayne and asked him to meet me on the parking lot of Angelique Plastiques. I then called the police again and told them that Wayne was the person who had tried to kill you and that they could catch him on that parking lot.

"When I checked with the police later last night, they said that Wayne didn't show up on the parking lot. They found his damaged car somewhere. He is driving a rental car now." Sarah paused and looked with concern at Tom, who had been patiently listening to her narrative.

"I guess that's how things stand at the moment," she continued. "I gave the police Wayne's cell phone number in hope that they could track him using triangulation of the cell phone signal. He is ungodly lucky, though, so I doubt that they have captured him yet."

Tom sighed. "There has certainly been a lot going on that I didn't know about," he said. "Until Mr. Alma visited my office, I never suspected that you were involved with another man."

"I'm so sorry, Tom. I wish that I could go back in time and do things differently. I can't, though, so I hope that you can forgive me. If you can't now, maybe sometime in the future you will be able." She hesitated, then added, "Please don't divorce me. The Catholic Church is against divorce. Our parents have had wonderful marriages. I think that we can work our way through this and have a wonderful marriage, too."

Sarah had been trying to read his expression, which never changed much. She was so afraid that he would leave her, and she felt so guilty that she again began to cry.

Tom was alarmed to see a look of utter desolation on the face of the woman whom he loved. Casting aside his anger and hurt feelings, he sought to console her. Tom hugged her and kissed her on the cheek.

"Don't despair, Sarah. I'm not going to divorce you. This wound to our marriage can be healed. I forgive you. We are human and have a tendency to sin. Jesus and Mary are the only two persons who never committed a sin."

Sarah felt so relieved that she felt her entire body relax. Tom was not going to leave her.

"Tom, I am now completely committed to our marriage. I'm open to whatever God wills for us. I'm in the boat and setting out into the deep. No more holding back."

"Do you love me, Sarah?"

"Yes. I truly do. When we were married, I just liked you a lot. However, my feelings for you deepened every month after we got married. I didn't realize that I was falling in love with you, but I was. Ironically, it was that idiot Wayne who made me finally understand that I was in love with you. When he suggested killing you, I realized how terrible it would be to lose you. I wanted to be your wife for the rest of my life on earth and to be with you for all eternity in Heaven."

"That's quite a commitment." Tom looked at her with such warmth that Sarah knew that all would be well.

"I hope that you don't have any more surprises for me today," Tom added with a slight grin.

"Poor Tom," Sarah said. "You would probably need to start taking heart medication if I shock you any more today. At the moment, I don't recall any additional shocking revelations, but I'll let you know if I think of anything else."

"I'll be fortifying myself so that I'm ready."

"You'd better, Mister!"

Late in the afternoon, Tom approached Sarah in the kitchen. She turned and smiled at him.

"I started cooking a pot roast a little while ago, and I just put some potatoes in. Dinner won't be ready for about two hours. Do you want a snack?"

"No, I'll just wait until dinner to eat. It occurred to me a few minutes ago that all of our neighbors already have their Christmas decorations up. We are apparently the slowpokes on the block. I just brought up three box of decorations from the basement, so I'm going to start putting our stuff up."

"Great. I'll help you."

Tom and Sarah decided to first put up the Christmas tree. They removed all of the branches from the box, grouped together the color-coded branches by length, and then inserted the branches into designated rows. In a short while, the seven-foot-high tree with snow-tipped branches was in position in the bay window in the living room.

They then put multi-colored lights on the tree followed by some garland and tinsel. It was time for the ornaments. Tom and Sarah each had many of their ornaments from their childhood tree. Their parents had more than enough ornaments for their own tree, so they had allowed their children to take any ornaments that they wanted.

Tom's ornaments included a Santa Claus, Mrs. Claus, elves, a gingerbread house, and some other the Peanuts characters including Charlie Brown, Snoopy, Lucy, and Linus.

Sarah's ornaments also included some elves, including three elves seated on small wreaths that the elves used as swings. She had several angel ornaments, a Nativity scene ornament, and a three wise men ornament. Sarah had a large illuminated angel that they placed on top of the tree.

They placed two animated figures near the fireplace. The first figure was Santa Claus handing a present to a little girl. The second figure was an elf building a toy train. The elf's hammer moved back and forth, making light contact with a nail protruding from the train.

"At that rate of impact, it's going to take that elf about a hundred years to get that nail completely into the train," Tom observed.

"A hundred years might be a bit optimistic actually," Sarah laughed. "He only gets to work on the train for one month per year. The other eleven months he is in the basement unplugged."

Sarah and Tom went to work on the outdoor decorations. A couple of weeks earlier Tom had purchased three giant inflatable decorations. On the front lawn they placed an inflatable igloo with a penguin on top, a snowman and penguin who rotated in circles around a Christmas tree in a transparent snowglobe, and a Peanuts-themed snowglobe that had Charlie Brown, Snoopy, and Woodstock on a sled.

"You are quite a Charlie Brown fan, aren't you?" Sarah chuckled as they watched this snowglobe inflate and the snowstorm inside begin.

"I am," Tom agreed.

"I have to admit that I am, too. As a kid, I used to watch 'A Charlie Brown Christmas' every December."

"So did I. And every October I would watch 'It's the Great Pumpkin, Charlie Brown'. I could always identify with Linus and see myself sitting in that pumpkin patch waiting for the Great Pumpkin."

"And I would be like Sally sitting next to you in the pumpkin patch."

After all three inflatables had been tethered into position, Tom and Sarah placed some light sculptures in the windows and on the lawn. On the front porch, they placed a Nativity scene that included the Holy Family and the three wise men.

"Whew, that was a lot of work!" Tom declared as they finished their work.

"I hope that you didn't overdue it," Sarah said with some concern. "You just got out of the hospital this morning. Perhaps we shouldn't have done all of this is one day."

"It's okay. I'm fine. It was a lot of fun. This is our first Christmas together."

"The first of many!" Sarah declared, giving him a hug.

They went inside and turned on the display, then stepped back out onto the front porch in order to admire their handiwork.

"Our display will use so much electricity that we'll probably overload the power grid and cause a blackout for the whole neighborhood," Sarah said.

"Oh, that would make us popular," Tom said with wry humor.

"The roast should be done by now." Sarah remarked as they went back inside. "Why don't you relax for a few minutes while I get dinner on the table?"

"Sounds great." Tom went in search of the novel that he had been reading earlier in the day.

CHAPTER 18

Shortly after they finished eating dinner, they went into the study in order to work on Christmas cards. Sarah wrote a personalized greeting on each card while Tom addressed the envelopes.

"I'm going to the kitchen to get a Dr. Pepper," Tom said after they had completed about twenty cards. "Do you want anything?"

"Yeah, bring me a soda, too."

At that moment, Tom and Sarah were startled to see a figure appear in the doorway. They both stood up.

"Well, aren't you two the cutest couple?" Wayne said mockingly as he entered the study.

Tom instantly recognized the malevolent visage of the man who had tried to kill him yesterday with a car.

"What are doing here?" Tom asked.

"Hasn't Sarah told you about me? She and I are old friends. In fact, I have known her for about two years longer than you have. We are very close. Tell Tommy Boy about how close we are, baby."

"How did you get in this house, Wayne?" Sarah asked.

"It was easy. I'm surprised that you don't have a burglar alarm system. I broke in through your patio doors."

"Then you can leave that same way by going out through those patio doors," Sarah told him. "Get out of here, Wayne."

"Now that's not a nice way to welcome me to your home, baby." He opened his jacket and rested his hand casually on the handle of the knife in his belt sheath. "I'm very disappointed in you, Sarah. It took me a while to figure it out. Do you think that I'm stupid? Didn't you know that I would figure it out?"

"Figure out what?"

"You set me up. You told the police about the China white in my apartment. Then you tried to lure me into a trap at the Angelique parking lot."

"You've been taking too many of your own drugs, Wayne. They are warping your brain. If you are going to be a drug dealer, you shouldn't be consuming all of your own product. You will never turn a profit that way."

Wayne laughed unpleasantly, clearly not amused. "I'll keep that in mind, baby. Anyway, you will be glad to hear that I am going to forgive you for betraying me to the police. And I'm even going to make you a millionaire. I'm here to give you another chance. We can kill Tommy Boy here and then split his money fifty-fifty."

"Go to Hell, Wayne," Sarah said.

"That is not the response that I was hoping for, baby."

"I'm not your baby. I am Thomas Angelique's wife, and I love him. I never want to see you again. Get out of here now!"

"I will leave when I'm ready to leave." Wayne pulled the knife out of its belt sheath.

"You will leave now." Tom grabbed a saber that was leaning against the wall behind the desk.

Wayne snickered. "How stupid do you think that I am, Tommy Boy? That is a fencing sword and has a blunt tip so that no one gets injured during your little fencing matches."

"Actually, this is an antique weapon whose blade and tip are very sharp. I thought that you might come here. Earlier today I removed this saber from the display case so that it would be ready in case you decided to pay us a visit."

"And here I am! But your little sword is as worthless as a butter knife! You should have bought a handgun if you want to defend your wife."

"I do have a handgun, but unfortunately it is not within reach at the moment."

Wayne laughed. "That's bad luck for you! But you've got style, dude. I like that." He stepped forward, gripping the knife more tightly. "I'm still going to kill you, but I'm not going to enjoy it as much as I thought that I would."

Wayne lunged at Tom, slashing at him with the knife. As Tom deftly evaded the blade, he countered with two quick strikes with his saber.

"Damn!" Wayne screamed and staggered backward, dropping the knife. Blood appeared where the sword had cut across his arm and chest.

Tom moved forward, keeping the sword pointed at Wayne. "We are going to call the police now. I want you to sit down on the floor there until they arrive. Your wounds are superficial; the paramedics will treat them."

Wayne pulled the Glock pistol out of the shoulder holster beneath his jacket. He aimed it at Tom's chest.

"That wasn't nice of you, Tommy Boy! I heard that you were a nice guy! I guess that Sarah was lying to both of us!"

Tom lowered the sword. "There is no need for this situation to escalate. If you leave now, we won't press charges against you. Just leave us alone and go live your own life."

"Thanks, Tommy Boy. I guess that I was wrong; you are a nice guy after all. But, since you cut me up, I will enjoy killing you very much."

Wayne's arm muscles tightened as he started to squeeze the trigger.

"No!" Sarah shouted and hurled herself between the gun and her husband.

"No, Sarah!" Tom yelled, not wanting her to make that sacrifice.

The bullet pierced her right side and blood poured forth. The impact sent her reeling onto the desk, scattering papers everywhere.

Sarah saw all this as she fell flat onto the desk. As she slid off the desk onto the floor, she remained conscious long enough to see the conclusion of the fight.

Wayne adjusted the aim of the gun in order to hit Tom with the next shot. However, as he pulled the trigger this second time, Tom was lunging forward with a saber thrust. She heard the explosion of the Glock pistol firing a second time.

Wayne aimed the shot at Tom's heart while Tom made a lunging thrust with his sword at Wayne's heart. Wayne missed, but Tom did not. Wayne died very soon after the sword impaled his heart.

Time seemed to change into slow motion as Sarah landed on the carpet. She saw blood spurt from her wound. Her mind filled with surrealistic images, reminding her of Salvador Dali paintings that she had studied in college in an art history class.

She found herself falling to the floor of St. Faustina Church. The front doors of the church had been blown open by a powerful wind that blew through the church.

On the altar there was a huge Eucharistic host from which red and white beams of light radiated. She heard a voice in her mind, and she found herself responding to the voice.

"The wind blows cold and freezes the land. Does thou seek not warmth?"

"Thy grace is sufficient for me," Sarah replied.

"The sun is setting as the day departs. Does thou seek not light?"

"The light of Thy face is sufficient for me."

"Your blood flows from you. Does thou seek not life?"

"Your life sustains me, and I live through your Body and Blood."

"So be it. Then live through me, with me, and in me."

"So be it," she agreed.

The red and white beams of light radiating from the Eucharistic host on the altar became so bright that the world seemed to be immersed in a sea of light. Sarah fell into a deep sleep.

Hours later, Sarah felt a kiss on her forehead. For a moment, she was unsure whether this was part of the vision or whether she was regaining consciousness.

She opened her eyes to find herself in unfamiliar surroundings. I'm in the hospital, she realized. She smiled. And there is Tom.

Tom returned her smile. "You looked like Sleeping Beauty there, so I decided to awaken you with a kiss."

"My Prince Charming."

"To tell you the truth, I think that you were starting to wake up on your own a few seconds before I kissed you."

"I have no idea how long I've been unconscious."

"About fifteen hours. After the ambulance got you here to the emergency room, they removed the bullet. Fortunately, it didn't hit your heart or lungs or any other vital organs. The doctor said that you will be fine."

"Good." Sarah glanced toward the chair in which a small figure was seated. "Chloe! I'm so glad to see you!"

Chloe beamed a smile at her. "Tom and I have been praying for you, Sarah. And your parents were praying with us, too."

"My parents?"

"Yes," Tom said. "They were here all day. About a half-hour ago, they went to get something to eat. They'll be back in a little while."

"They must have been worried sick," Sarah said. "After I was shot, I thought that I was going to die. I am surprised that I am still alive. While I was unconscious, I had a profound experience of God's mercy." She described the vision to Tom and Chloe. "This has been a night and day of mercy."

"Sarah, do you remember my riddle about what sea is deeper and vaster than both the Pacific and Atlantic oceans?" Chloe's eyes twinkled as she posed the question.

"Yes, what is the answer?" Sarah asked.

"We are constantly immersed in an infinite ocean of God's mercy. Be open to receive His mercy."

"I will be open to it," Sarah promised. "I understand it now. I realize that on the cross, the fountain of God's mercy was opened by the lance in the side of Jesus. From His heart, a living fountain of mercy flows."

"I apparently married a mystic," Tom said.

"You married a very selfish, foolish young woman," she said. "However, I am not now what I was then. You can trust me completely."

"I believe you."

She looked at Tom and felt as though she was truly seeing him for the first time. I love this man and everything about him. I love all his quirks, his crazy inner ear that keeps him from flying, his allergies, his funny imitations of famous persons as well as his kindness, courage, and compassion. Talk about paradigm shifts, she thought smiling broadly.

"Are you okay?" he asked, puzzled by her expression.

"I have never been better, my Prince, never better."

"I'm glad, my beautiful Snow Maiden," he said and kissed his beloved wife.

As a satisfied grin spread across her face, Chloe leaned back in her chair and folded her arms. It is just like in a fairy tale, she reflected contentedly. And they lived happily ever after.

978-0-595-44644-5
0-595-44644-2